Haven Hill

Haven Hill

DAISY LUTHER

BANNED BOOKS PUBLISHING
CHEYENNE, WYOMING

This book is dedicated to my daughters.
I'm so very proud of the women that both of you
have become.
Love,
Mom

Disclaimer

This novel is a work of fiction. The characters and events come from the author's imagination and are not intended to depict any actual person or real-life situation. Any resemblance to real individuals, living or dead, or to real events is coincidental.

Chapter 1

Kate Lindsey checked her list as she jammed the last bag into the back of the very full, yellow, two-door Jeep. The piece of paper had come from the cheery, frog-covered pad currently attached to her refrigerator with magnets. It read, *Would you like flies with that?*

Today, the lime-green sheet had every box neatly checked off beside the items she'd loaded into the Jeep. Kate was officially ready for a calm, relaxing getaway to her favorite place in the world.

Her fourteen-year-old daughter, Ariel, leaned her lanky frame against the passenger door, face glued to the phone that was perpetually glued to her hand. Kate opened her mouth to say something, then decided not to. Soon enough, they'd reach their destination, and there was no phone service there. It would be a self-resolving problem. *Pick your battles*, she thought.

"Can you please go make sure all the doors and windows are locked? It looks like we're ready to go," she said.

Ariel pushed herself off the Jeep, eyes still locked on her screen. Her long chocolate-brown braids were gathered with colorful scrunchies, and she wore a yellow T-shirt proclaiming More Spaghetti, Less Upsetty over cut-off jean shorts. She was at that age where she was all long limbs and awkward angles, moving in a blend of grace and clumsiness that was uniquely teenaged.

Kate forced herself to look away so she wouldn't bark at Ariel to put down the freaking phone and watch where she was going.

Instead, she focused on the Jeep. Kate enjoyed being self-reliant, and she'd spent a lot of time learning to handle basic maintenance. She topped off the washer fluid, breathing in the sharp bite of the blue liquid.

Just as Ariel returned, Kate slammed the hood down and flipped the latches into place with a thud. Perfect timing.

Ariel hopped into the Jeep, wincing as the few inches of her bare legs below her shorts met the hot leather seat. "Hot, hot, hot!" she chanted, lifting her rear and grabbing the beach towel they kept on the floorboard for exactly this purpose. Once settled, she shot her mother an impish grin. "Starbucks? Pretty please with a whole bunch of sugar on top?"

Kate laughed. "Don't you mean a whole bunch of sugar in the cup?"

They pulled out of the driveway and drove a couple of blocks to the drive-thru. Once their giant frappuccinos were safely in the cup holders, Kate plugged her phone into the dashboard and selected a playlist titled Loud Road Trip. Ariel cranked up the volume, and they sped toward the highway, their dark hair flying behind them like flags in a stout breeze as Jim Morrison hoarsely urged them to "let it roll, baby, roll."

Between the music and the wind streaming through the topless Jeep, conversation was impossible. They rode in agreeable silence, breaking into loud, terrible singing whenever Janis Joplin started bemoaning the loss of another little piece of her heart. They laughed at how awful they sounded.

Kate's heart squeezed every time she glanced at her daughter—purple braces, scattered freckles, the fragile beauty of a kid hovering between girl and woman. Not long ago, she had nearly lost her girl, and some instinct still flinched at shadows.

She cut off the thought and shook her shoulders, physically shedding the dark memory. She was determined to focus on the here and now—the joy of spending time with her snarky, clever teenager at their cabin in the North Carolina mountains.

After a couple of hours, the gigantic frappuccinos demanded attention, so Kate pulled the Jeep into a rest area. Ariel hopped out and raced toward the bathrooms. Kate hurried after her. Though years of therapy had helped them both, she doubted she'd ever be truly okay letting Ariel out of her sight again.

Ariel rolled her eyes when she stepped out of the stall and saw Kate leaning against the counter.

"Mom, I can use the bathroom by myself!"

"I know. I potty-trained you," Kate said, sticking out her tongue. She tried to be cool, but her mind always raced with what could go wrong for a young girl alone in a place like this.

Ariel wheedled some money from her and bought a pack of peanut M&Ms from the vending machine, then they were back on the road.

"We haven't been to the cabin since early summer," Ariel said. "Do you think everything's okay there?"

"It should be." Kate furrowed her brow. "Mr. Slocum's been stopping by once a week, and he'd have called to let us know if something was wrong." Their grizzled neighbor treated them like family, looking after the place in exchange for a few sociable meals around the fire pit.

"I can't wait to lie in the hammock and read my book."

"It's not all fun and games this trip," Kate warned. "We have to clean, stock the cabin with supplies, do inventory, and make sure all our systems are in good working order."

Things in the news had been nuts lately—a highly contested recent election, protests occurring almost weekly, sometimes just blocks from their apartment. Every week, they escalated in volume and vandalism, even though the media still called them "mostly peaceful."

Maybe that was why Kate carried a constant undertow of stress. She wanted to be sure they had a safe place to go if they needed to leave the city.

Years ago, when she'd first started preparing for hard times and emergencies, she'd bought the small, dilapidated cabin and its wooded acreage. She and Ariel had spent many weekends there, and Kate was proud of the work she'd done to turn it into a viable bug-out spot and, surprisingly, their favorite place to go on vacation. Aside from Ariel and Mr. Slocum, the only other person who knew about the cabin was her exboyfriend—something she deeply regretted. But he wasn't in any position to come back here, and the weight on her shoulders eased as the terrain grew more mountainous and the roads more wooded.

She always felt safe at the cabin in the foothills. She'd named her little property Haven Hill.

Kate turned onto a gravel road and wound through a heavily wooded stretch dotted with a few homes. After a few bumpy minutes, the houses disappeared.

"Good thing we stopped to pee," Ariel said, as she always did. "Otherwise, this road would shake it out of us!"

Kate laughed, as *she* always did, and turned onto a barely noticeable dirt trail, driving a hundred yards to the gate. She switched off the music so they could soak in the forest sounds—birds, a distant creek, and the distant tinkling of the windchimes she'd hung.

Kate eyed the chain across the gate. It looked just as they'd left it. Ariel grabbed the key from the tiny hook on the dashboard and hopped out to unlock it.

The familiar forest around them glowed with early-autumn color—yellows, reds, and olive tones blending into a warm cacophony. The smell of the woods enveloped them, earthy and piney and moss-rich. It was noticeably cooler here than in the city, and Kate relished the crisp mountain air.

Something in the stillness made her pause. Not fear—just the awareness of how isolated they truly were. How separate from the rest of the world.

It was comforting.

Mostly.

She put the Jeep in gear and drove through, waiting while Ariel relocked the gate. They followed their private road up to the cabin. The peace of the area stole their words once they closed the gate between them and the world. They crossed a narrow, rustic bridge, and the Jeep began the climb up the hill.

Finally, they rounded a sharp corner and leveled out. There was the cabin.

It had once been more of a shack than a cabin, but over the years Kate had insulated it, added a propane tank, installed a woodstove insert in the old stone fireplace, and replaced the windows and doors one by one. She'd learned an entire skill set renovating the place, spending about 200 hours on YouTube to do so, and she was delighted with how it had turned out.

Now it was an eclectic little building surrounded by windchimes, brightly painted birdhouses, and perennial beds. A cheerful green metal roof topped it. Echinacea still bloomed, its purple petals bright against the weathered wood and vivid pink shutters. Stained-glass pieces they'd scavenged from flea markets hung in most of the windows. The place was entirely theirs—designed to spark joy with its colors, views, and the music of the creek below.

Ariel whooped and jumped out of the Jeep the instant it rolled to a stop.

This place had held them through the worst days of their lives. The woods, the creek, the colors... it all wrapped around them like a quilt. Here, they were safe from the dangers and stress of the city.

Kate pulled the parking brake and removed the keys.

She took a moment to revel in the quirky beauty of their refuge. A grin spread across her face as her shoulders relaxed the rest of the way. The keys jingled, the lock clicked open, and her lavender-painted front door welcomed them home, to their Haven.

Chapter 2

Inside, the cabin looked exactly as it always did. The sameness gave them a sense of permanence and safety, and Kate felt that familiar, peculiar rush of satisfaction that everything was still exactly where she had left it. Sheets covered the upholstered furniture to keep the dust off. After months of being closed up, the air held a musty, stale weight.

"Weird. It almost smells like someone was smoking in here," Ariel said, wrinkling her nose.

Kate inhaled deeply. Ariel was right; there was a faint, smoky edge beneath the dust. Kate shrugged it off. "Probably just from the wood stove."

Without discussion, they immediately set about opening windows to let the forest breeze sweep through like the world's best air freshener.

Kate stepped onto the back lean-to porch to flip the main breaker, feeling the faint buzz as electricity hummed to life. She was lucky—municipal power had already been installed by the previous owner, saving her a fortune. End of the world or not, she was a huge fan of electricity for as long as she could have it.

She walked back in, clicking on ceiling fan switches as she went. She'd found four palm-leaf-style fans at

Habitat for Humanity years ago and had grabbed them immediately. They added both a welcome breeze and the slightly quirky character she loved.

The walls were whitewashed, and the late-afternoon sun shone through the windows, the stained glass scattering soft jewel tones across the wood. The cabin's main room held their living room, dining area, and—Kate's favorite—their little library. Ariel, a history-and-literature nerd after her own heart, liked to call it The Great Hall. The kitchen was a small, cheery room with a large open pass-through window cut into the wall. Two small bedrooms and a simple bathroom completed the layout, the bathroom cobbled together from whatever fixtures had come with the cabin and the bright, mismatched tiles Kate had scavenged from Habitat.

With the windows open and the fans whirling, the room began to smell of pine needles and old books. Since the cabin had no television, no phone service, and no internet, the wall of shelves served as both entertainment and old-fashioned Google.

Kate loved her books: vintage herbal guides, brightly photographed plant-ID references, and the eclectic novels they devoured together. Each summer, she brought up more boxes, and somehow, there was always room to squeeze them in. They'd spent countless evenings reading yard-sale paperbacks in front of the fire, wrapped in mismatched afghans that had been thrown carelessly across the sofas.

Ariel flopped onto the secondhand lavender couch, its springs groaning in protest.

"Home, sweet home!" she crowed, grinning wide enough to flash both dimples and braces.

"Let's get everything inside before dark and then make some dinner," Kate said, in a tone that placed it firmly between suggestion and decree.

Ariel rolled her eyes but rose without complaint.

They unloaded the cooler, groceries, overnight bags, and the other goods they'd packed precariously into the Jeep. While Ariel tucked the refrigerated items into the funky yellow vintage fridge, Kate reattached the Jeep's soft top in case of rain. The waxed canvas resisted her with its usual stubbornness, but after straining, zipping, and wrestling Velcro into place, the vehicle was storm-ready.

"Campfire dinner?" Ariel asked when she returned, batting her lashes dramatically and thwacking her elbow on the bookshelf without missing a beat.

Kate snorted a laugh. "Sure."

Soon they'd gathered everything for an easy, satisfying dinner. They were both starving after the drive, so hot dogs and s'mores it would be, plus a tub of coleslaw Kate had brought from home—her token attempt at adding a vegetable. She pulled buns, ketchup, and mustard from the fridge. Ariel assembled marshmallows, chocolate, peanut butter, and graham crackers, practically vibrating with anticipation.

"You build the fire, kiddo," Kate said. Ariel needed to keep her skills sharp. One never knew.

Ariel stacked wood into a tidy teepee and lit a twist of newspaper beneath it. Within minutes, a proper fire was crackling, sparks skipping upward as Kate added larger pieces.

Kate went back inside to doctor the buns and get the hot dogs, returning with two paper plates laden with the components of the feast.

The air was cooling as the sun drifted lower. Ariel ducked inside to grab hoodies.

For a moment, Kate thought she heard something move through the trees. Her hand drifted instinctively to the small of her back, confirming the familiar weight of her pistol. But it was likely only a squirrel or a deer.

They slid the tines of long roasting forks through their hot dogs, and soon, the smell of sizzling meat drifted into the evening. Kate touched her Glock again—habit, preparation, instinct. Delicious smells could draw all kinds of visitors.

Four stumps ringed the fire pit as makeshift stools, and they each claimed one, cooking their hot dogs to their preferred level of crispness. By the time their first course was ready, the sun had slipped below the trees, and a dusky purple light washed across the clearing.

They relocated to their far more comfortable Adirondack chairs a little farther from the heat and ate without talking. Both introverts, they were perfectly content in silence. Only the crackling fire and the rustle of the forest filled the air.

Kate felt the last of the tension melt from her shoulders as she bit into her hot dog, perfectly charred at the edges. She leaned back in her chair, chewing and savoring, watching Ariel inhale her food like she was preparing for hibernation. Oh, to have the metabolism of a fourteen-year-old.

Their hunger satisfied, they lingered, waiting for stomachs to settle before moving on to dessert.

"I love it here, Mom," Ariel said softly. "I always feel safe—like nothing bad can happen at Haven Hill." She tucked her long legs up and rested her chin on her knees, eyes on the flames.

Kate smiled, but something in her chest tugged, a superstitious little wince. Bad things could happen anywhere—they both knew that too well. Saying everything was fine always felt like tempting fate. But Ariel didn't need worry tonight. She needed peace.

"Anyplace can be safe if you have the skills to protect yourself," Kate reminded her gently. "And you do."

Ariel nodded and raced back to the cabin to get the components of dessert.

Upon her return, she began skewering as many marshmallows as physics would allow onto her roasting stick. Kate took that as her cue to prepare the S'mores: the secret ingredient, a thin layer of peanut butter, spread across the crackers. Chocolate squares went down next, and she waited while Ariel hovered maternally over her marshmallows, roasting them to a charred-black perfection. Kate preferred hers golden brown.

Three years ago, Kate had pulled Ariel out of school, homeschooling her with a curriculum that blended academics with outdoor survival, marksmanship, and self-defense. She wanted Ariel to be empowered, confident, and capable. Together they'd taken courses, hiked countless weekends, and trained in Krav Maga twice a week. Their education had been unconventional—pairing foraging with botany, canning with chemistry, animal scat with biology—but Ariel thrived. She was intelligent, curious, and fiercely self-sufficient.

Kate was proud of the girl she'd become. Proud of both of them, really, for clawing their way from trauma to competence. She chuckled inwardly; their therapist had probably bought a new car on their dime.

Worth every penny.

"Mom?" Ariel asked tentatively as she positioned a molten marshmallow onto each chocolate square and pressed another peanut-buttered cracker on top. "Do you think I could go back to regular school in September?"

They'd been inseparable for three years. Kate had known that this moment was coming. "We can discuss it," she said lightly, even as every instinct in her screamed no, no, no.

"I just want to hang out with my friends again," Ariel said. "I want to be normal."

It was time, and they both knew it.

"When we get back, we'll see about getting you registered," Kate said with a bright, practiced smile.

Ariel wasn't fooled. She laid a gentle hand on her mother's arm. "It'll be okay, Mom. All that stuff is over."

Kate nodded, her smile fixed. She hoped her daughter was right. She truly did. But safety, she'd learned, was never a guarantee.

They ate gooey, perfect S'mores until they were smeared with peanut butter and chocolate, laughing at how ridiculous they looked. When they'd finished, they gathered the trash, tossing their paper plates and napkins into the fire. Kate scooped sand into the fire pit and set the lid on top to smother the flames.

They made their way back to the cabin, overly full and relaxed.

Inside, the refrigerator door hung wide open.

"Ariel, you've got to shut the fridge all the way or the food will spoil."

"I did shut it," Ariel insisted, defensive and certain.

"Maybe it opened itself," Kate said, half-joking, half-weary. The fridge was ancient—maybe the seal was finally failing. She tested the door a few times; it seemed fine. She ran a finger along the gasket, frowned, then shrugged. She was tired. It could be tomorrow's problem. She dragged a dining chair with chipped green paint in front of the fridge to hold it closed.

It had been a long day, and they washed their roasting forks and dishes through half-closed eyelids.

"Night, Mom," Ariel said, hugging Kate a little longer than usual. "I love you."

Kate squeezed her tightly. "I love you too, sweetie. Sleep well."

When Ariel disappeared into her room, Kate stared out into the dark forest surrounding the cabin. A sharp snap of a branch made her jump, her breath catching. She listened hard—nothing followed. Just a squirrel, she told herself.

Everything is peaceful, she reminded herself, taking a long, steady breath.

They were safe. They were at Haven Hill.

Chapter 3

When Ariel woke, she heard soft clunking coming from the main room of the cabin. Her mother muttered something unintelligible as she worked, and Ariel smothered a little giggle. She wasn't surprised that her mom was up way earlier than she was – she was always up at the crack of dawn. And, Mom also liked to talk to herself.

It was going to be a good day at the cabin, Ariel was convinced with her usual bright optimism. She hoped she would be able to sneak in some book time – she was deeply engrossed in a mystery from the library where the girl was the hero and was preparing to save herself. It was her all-time favorite kind of book.

She stretched luxuriously, her long, skinny arms reaching for the ceiling and her toes pointing off the bed. She stretched so big and so hard she couldn't hear a thing for the moment, and it was a fantastically satis-fying stretch.

She loved staying at the cabin. She'd left her window open, and the air in her room smelled fresh and piney. She could hear the birds and the distant rushing of the creek down the hill behind them. She could listen to it for hours — if she didn't have to pee so badly.

Reluctantly, she got up from her comfy bed to go to the bathroom, then joined her mom.

...

Kate sat cross-legged on the floor just outside the pantry, surrounded by canned goods, her favorite hot pink cabin coffee mug steaming on the bottom shelf in front of her. She jotted down her inventory in a colorful notebook and sorted out the remaining goods by date. The boxes of canned goods she'd brought with them went into the back of the pantry, and any cans with a "best by" date within the next year went back into those same boxes to go home with them and get used up.

She smiled when her daughter emerged from the bathroom, wearing an enormous purple-and-yellow T-shirt and her long dark hair sticking out wildly in all directions.

Barefoot, Ariel padded over to join her mom on the floor. "How goes the inventory?" she asked, even though she really wasn't that interested in canned food.

"Pretty good," Kate replied with far more enthusiasm about the topic. "We're leaving behind more than we're taking back, so our food supply here is growing. But I did think we had more canned ravioli in the pantry. I wrote it down right here the last time we were at the cabin." Kate frowned at her notepad. Had she forgotten to mark down that they'd used five cans of it since the last inventory? She didn't like it when the numbers didn't match. It meant something was off — and she hated things that were off. She put the brakes on her rampant thoughts. She was probably overthinking a simple miscalculation. "Anyway, are you hungry?"

Ariel looked at her like she was crazy. "Um...YES. When am I *not* hungry?"

Kate laughed and got up to make some scrambled eggs and toast for both of them. They took their plates of breakfast out to the vivid, teal-colored rocking chairs on the screened-in back porch.

A symphony of the forest played as though the very mountain was welcoming them back with a serenade. The birds sang energetically, the sound of the creek was even louder, and a breeze through the treetops played backup. Kate thought this was the most peaceful sound in the world, and she relished sitting in silence with her daughter.

Ariel was the first to speak.

"What's on the agenda today?"

Kate referred to the notebook she'd brought outside.

"I've done the canned food inventory. We've got to go down to the basement and check on the supplies down there, then I thought we could take a hike and cool off in the creek. Sound good?"

"I wish the basement wasn't so creepy," Ariel complained.

"Well, it's a basement. Basements are always creepy. It's the nature of basements. You're helping," Kate informed her pointedly.

Ariel sighed deeply, pretending to be horribly inconvenienced. "I had plans to lollygag and carry out shenanigans."

Kate grinned. "Well, you've been bamboozled. I'm discombobulating your plans, whippersnapper."

"I'm flabbergasted by this malarkey, you flibbertigibbet."

"Are we about to have a kerfuffle or a brouhaha?"

Ariel thought for a minute. "Darn it, I can't think of any more good words. It's too early."

Laughing, they took their plates inside and split up to get dressed for the busy day ahead.

...

Ariel made her way down the creaky wooden stairs from the kitchen into the basement. It smelled damp down there, but not altogether unpleasant. Her mom had heroically cleared the spiderwebs, so she didn't have to walk into any and do the spiderweb dance to frantically get the sticky silk off her face.

Working together, they managed to replace batteries, count water jugs, and test their gear in just an hour.

Ariel stomped up the steps loudly, bellowing enthusiastically, "Hiking time!!!"

Kate shook her head, smiling, and made her way up at a slightly less exuberant pace. "Do you want to eat here or while we're out?"

"Out!"

Once they were both dressed in T-shirts and shorts over swimsuits, the two quickly gathered up some snacks to throw into their backpacks, which were otherwise ready to go and equipped with personal water filters, knives, bear spray, paracord, extra socks, and other essentials for a day in the forest. Kate patted the small of her back to ensure that her pistol was holstered there, and added a couple of extra magazines of ammunition to her own bag.

"Can't I take some water from here?" Ariel pleaded.

Kate shook her head. "There's perfectly fine water in that creek down there, and you know how to make it safe to drink. What happens if you don't use skills?"

Ariel sighed deeply, rolled her eyes, and answered in a singsong voice, "You lose them."

They each clipped a set of "bear bells" to their belt loops. Most of the time, bears wanted to avoid you as much as you wanted to avoid them. The jangling of the bells was just an early warning system to alert them to your presence. Kate had made theirs from leftover Christmas sleigh bell ornaments and then added a carabiner to attach them to belt loops or backpacks.

Kate locked the door and rattled the doorknob, checking it as they left. Ariel looked at her like she was crazy. She teased, "Who are you locking out, exactly? The bears? The raccoons? Maybe those scary, scary squirrels?"

"It's just good security," Kate informed her. "And one never knows when the squirrels will band together with the raccoons and wreak all sorts of havoc. Which path do you want to take?"

"Let's go up to the bridge and then come back and swim."

The bridge wasn't actually a bridge at all. It was a huge tree that had conveniently fallen over the rushing creek, providing them with a safe, dry passage. It was a twenty-minute walk to get there, and they set out at a comfortable pace, the bells jingling softly, merrily as they walked.

The blackberry bushes that lined the narrow trail were bursting with ripe fruit. Ariel crammed handfuls of berries into her mouth as they walked, groaning in delight as berry juice ran down her face. Kate shook her head and laughed, then grabbed a few sweet, ripe berries of her own to snack on.

When they reached the bridge, they went halfway across and sat down over the creek, swinging their legs as they grabbed another snack from their backpacks. When they finished, they each pulled out their personal water filters and got a satisfying drink from the fresh, cold mountain creek.

After their thirst was sated, they filtered water to take with them. Ariel could have done it in her sleep. She filled the bladder that came with the Sawyer Mini from the stream, holding a clean bandana over the opening to strain out leaves and grit. Then she screwed the filter onto the bladder, flipped it upside down, and squeezed. Clear water ran through the filter and into her bottle—cool, clean, and safe to drink.

Kate insisted on wandering around the little clearing so she could quiz Ariel on the plants in the area. The mulberries and elderberries weren't quite ripe, but they would be soon. The bright red sumac berries were ready to be harvested and ground into a bright seasoning.

An abundance of chickweed was ready for salad. Wood nettle leaves (which were far less painful to harvest than their cousins, stinging nettles) could be used as cooked greens or dried for tea. There was an enormous patch of burdock, and they pulled two apiece to peel and cook the roots for supper at the cabin.

Once they'd identified the edibles, the medicinals, and the do-not-eat-under-any-conditions flora and fungi, Kate gathered some wintergreen from the bright patch she'd located, and some of the chickweed, as well as wild onions that she'd use later with the burdock root.

By that time, Ariel was practically dancing with impatience to get going. Finally, at not–so–long last, they set off toward the swimming hole.

On the way there, they separated to practice walking as quietly as possible in the forest, using some tricks they had learned at an outdoor survival class they had taken together. Carefully placing their feet as they walked and avoiding the brush that grabbed at their clothing, they played one of their favorite forest games and tried to sneak up on one another without making a sound. Peals of laughter rang through their forest as they one-upped each other, and soon they made it to their next destination.

A narrow place in the creek beside a deeper section created a perfect, hidden swimming hole, a wonderful place to cool off on a hot day. They stripped off their hiking boots and socks, then put their outerwear on top before wading in. Ariel floated on her back while Kate lay on a rock at the edge of the swimming hole, gazing up at the bright blue sky trimmed with lacy autumn leaves.

She loved this place, too.

As she watched, the sky began to darken, and thunder rumbled in the distance, cutting their refreshing dip short. "Boooo," chorused Ariel, without any real heat.

Begrudgingly, they got out of the water and carried their bags, clothing, and boots across to the cabin side of the creek. They got dressed quickly, dry clothes over wet suits, and wandered up to the house, utterly relaxed.

Ariel made straight for the door.

"Wait! I have to unlock it," Kate yelled from behind, shaking her head and smiling at the girl's impatience.

Ariel turned to theatrically twist the doorknob anyway...

....and the door to the cabin swung open.

Kate felt her blood run cold. "Ariel! Get back here!"

Her daughter backed away from the open door, and the color drained from her face.

"I know you locked that door, Mom."

"I did," Kate nodded, her mind racing to devise a strategy.

The forest suddenly felt too quiet.

Too still.

Like it was listening.

"Let's just go," Ariel pleaded.

"We can't," Kate whispered.

"Why not?"

Kate felt like she'd swallowed a large rock that sat in her stomach.

"My Jeep keys are inside."

Chapter 4

They stood there for one suspended moment, frozen by fear, barely breathing. The cabin door hung open like a gaping wound.

Kate forced herself to inhale. The breath broke the paralysis.

"Ariel," she said quietly, steadily, "I need you to go hide behind the Jeep. No matter what happens, no matter what you hear, don't come in unless I say it's okay. If I'm not out in five minutes, you run down the trail and go to Mr. Slocum's."

"That's miles away!" Ariel's voice wavered. "I'm not leaving you. I can help—"

"Promise me." The edge in Kate's voice cut through the rising panic.

Ariel's chin trembled. Then she nodded and backed away.

Thunder cracked overhead as the sky split open, dumping rain so hard it blurred the treeline. Lightning flashed, reflecting off puddles that hadn't existed a minute earlier.

As Ariel disappeared behind the Jeep, Kate turned to the task at hand.

She drew her Glock from the holster at the small of her back. She racked the slide in a single, familiar motion. The sound steadied her.

Three years of training weren't just theory now. She thought of the structure-clearing class from that tactical retreat outside Vegas—hallways, corners, doorways, all drilled so many times they felt like reflex. She never truly believed she'd need it and had nearly skipped it in favor of a cool swim.

Today, she was really glad she hadn't skipped it.

Kate set her stance and focused on her breathing – long exhale, slow inhale. She needed her pulse under control. She needed her mind sharp.

"Go," she whispered to herself.

She pushed the door wide open, slamming it against the wall behind it.

Finger off the trigger until ready to fire, she mentally recited.

She slipped inside, back to the wall.

Low ready. Muzzle down.

The pistol dipped, then wobbled as she corrected it, conscious of every ounce in her grip.

Corners first. Pie, not hug. Peek. Sweep. Advance.

Lightning flickered outside, throwing jagged shadows across the living room.

She cleared the cabin room by room. She felt the pressure building with each peek, each turn, each room she entered.

Under the beds.

Inside the closets, she yanked the clothes to one side.

Her Glock felt heavy in her hand. Her arms started to tremble.

Behind the couch. Inside the tiny bathroom. Always keeping a wall at her back.

She slammed each window shut as she went, latching them.

She rechecked each one out of habit.

The basement door waited at the far end of the kitchen, darker than the rest of the room. She stopped a few feet away. Clearing a basement alone, during a storm, with her kid outside—that was not on today's agenda.

Instead, she slid the Molly bar into the steel brackets she'd installed last year. It bought time. Not perfection, but time. She shoved the heavy kitchen table against it, putting her shoulder into the push until the legs dug into the floorboards.

Good.

Her keys still hung on the hook by the front door, right where she had left them. That part was normal.

Everything else about this was anything *but* normal.

She shoved the thought aside and pocketed the keys.

Outside, Ariel waited in the downpour, soaked and shaking. Relief spread across the girl's face the instant she spotted Kate.

"It's okay," Kate said, trying to make it true. "Nobody's inside. Nothing looks disturbed." Then, she spoke softly, "Maybe I didn't lock the door right."

"You checked it," Ariel insisted. "You always check it."

"I know." Kate scanned the tree line, something tightening low in her stomach. "There has to be a rational explanation."

"I don't care. I just want to leave."

Kate nodded. "We're leaving."

They reentered the cabin together—shoulder to shoulder this time. "Grab anything quick," Kate told her. "We're not staying to pack."

Ariel scooped up the nearest bag. Kate shoved a box of Glock ammo into hers. She checked the windows one more time—every lock, every latch—then jammed a chair under the back doorknob.

When they got outside onto the porch, the rain was a solid sheet. The metal roof thundered above them. Kate rested one hand on Ariel's shoulder, her other hand holding the Glock high and tight, scanning the tree line as they sprinted to the Jeep.

Bags tossed in. Doors slammed. Locks engaged.

With relief, Kate turned the key.

Click.

Her heartbeat stuttered.

She tried again.

Click.

A cold, creeping dread seeped into her bones. She turned toward Ariel, forcing her expression neutral even as the girl's face went pale.

No words were needed.

They were trapped at the cabin, and both of them knew it.

...

Back inside, the roar of rain on the roof made conversation a shout. Ariel was shivering—not from cold, but from terror.

"This could be a coincidence," Kate said, hearing the strain in her own voice. "Things break. Doors don't always catch. It doesn't mean—"

"It's him," Ariel whispered so softly it couldn't be heard above the sounds of the storm, but Kate knew what she was saying. Tears streaked her cheeks. "I know it's him."

Kate felt something in her chest clench. "Honey, no. He's locked away for years."

"What if he got out?" Ariel's voice rose. "What if nobody told us?"

"The prosecutor would notify us. That was the agreement." But even as she said it, worry gnawed at her ribs. "Let's do a breathing exercise, okay? You remember how."

It took coaxing, but Ariel settled into the floral armchair, clutching the blanket Kate had crocheted for her. They breathed together—five in, five out—until Ariel's chest eased.

"Tell me something you hear," Kate said softly.

"The rain. And the windchimes."

"Something you feel."

"The velvet on the arms of the couch. The blanket."

"Something you see."

Ariel opened her eyes and blinked slowly. "The trees. The woodstove."

"And smell?"

A small, shaky smile. "My armpits are stinky."

Kate huffed a laugh—thank goodness for Ariel's sense of humor. "We'll put deodorant on the list."

Ariel wiped her eyes. "Mom...can we just walk to Mr. Slocum's?"

Kate looked at the storm pounding the windows. Lightning lit the woods like daylight for half a second. Thunder cracked so loud it shook dust from the rafters.

"Yes," she said gently. "But not tonight. The trail's slick, the rocks are a hazard, and the mud will be thick. We cannot risk getting hurt out there. It'll be safer in the daylight."

She forced a confident smile. "So. We make this place secure."

....

Kate snapped into motion. She needed to turn this little cabin into a hard target.

"First rule," she said. "We stay together. No exceptions."

They ran back out into the storm once more—Kate covering the perimeter with her flashlight and Glock while Ariel grabbed the bags and slammed the liftgate. Thirty seconds. That's all she allowed.

Back inside, Kate tossed Ariel a towel and wiped her own face.

"Doors first," she said. A sturdy barricade meant that even if someone managed to break through the locked door, they still had to get past the furniture in the way.

Together, they shoved the heavy stereo armoire against the front door until the legs dug grooves into the floor. The red-and-white Hoosier cabinet went against the back door.

Not perfect barricades. But better than nothing.

Kate pulled open the big bottom drawer in the kitchen, grabbed a hammer and a handful of long nails, and sat on a cutting board on the floor.

"What are you doing?" Ariel asked.

"Making caltrops."

"Is that like Cyclops's cousin?"

Kate giggled, even though she didn't really feel like it. "Sharp pointy things. Always pointy side up. If someone comes through a window, we'll hear the scream."

It took a few attempts, but soon she'd bent six nails into crude, spiked stars. Not elegant but effective. She placed half a dozen under each window, precisely where a foot would land when climbing in.

Next, she tackled the bedrooms. The smaller the space, the easier it was to defend, she had been taught, and it made a lot more sense now, in the moment. Kate dug through the hardware drawer and found some hook-and-eye closures she'd bought months ago. She mounted them on the exterior doors of both bedrooms and the bathroom. They weren't heavy-duty, but they'd slow someone down. Bear bells on each latch added an extra alarm.

The cabin was quieter now, except for the storm hammering the roof.

The basement door caught her eye again.

"I think I should clear the basement," she said, half to herself.

"No!" Ariel snapped, panic returning. "Mom, it's not safe."

"But what if someone's down there?"

"Then they can stay down there. If they get out, we'll hear it."

Kate stared at the door, thinking. The Molly bar and table barricade would slow someone, but not stop them.

Fine. Then she'd respond accordingly.

If someone tries to break through that door, she decided, *I shoot through it.*

That thought calmed her more than it scared her.

Plans always did.

She shut the blackout blinds in every room, cutting off the outside world. She turned off all but one reading lamp. She handed Ariel her book and grabbed one for herself.

The Glock sat on the table between them.

Kate tried to convince herself she'd overreacted. That the open door, the missing food, the old fridge popping open, the Jeep refusing to start—maybe it all had innocent explanations.

But her gut knew better.

Something was wrong.

This night would not pass quietly.

And Kate doubted she would sleep at all.

Chapter 5

Kate dozed fitfully in the armchair as the rain continued to fall. Now, thankfully, it was a soft, musical patter that always reminded her of those windchimes made of wood. It was the kind of sound you could fall asleep to, under piles of blankets, gently cushioned by soft pillows.

Every sound that wasn't the rain caused Kate to sit up and grab her pistol, instantly wide awake. An occasional tree branch falling in the forest sounded like gunshots. The plaintive call of some kind of animal in the woods sounded like someone screaming for help. An occasional gust of wind rattled the door in its frame, making her quite certain someone was about to burst through the door she'd so carefully barricaded.

However, the noises came and went without any unsettling causes. Still, sleep was elusive, and just after 5 am, Kate gave up on rest. She went to make some coffee and start her day, careful not to awaken her slumbering daughter. Ariel needed the rest and the respite from fear.

She got dressed, donning well-worn Levis, a dark graphic tee shirt, and a dark green and black plaid flannel shirt unbuttoned over it. She laced up her favorite hiking boots and braided her long dark hair. She was ready to face the day.

Kate sat on one of the kitchen chairs near the barricaded basement door with her notebook. The rain had given a reprieve, and now it felt oddly silent in the cabin without the sound of it on the roof. She didn't dare put on her headphones for some music, though. She needed all her senses to be sharp.

She was about to pack some pretty important bug-out bags, and she didn't want to forget anything.

Afterward, we're going to laugh at how much we overreacted, she told herself, certainly.

She jotted down the "pillars of preparedness" that she had learned about on a website, leaving space for notes. This was the best way she could think of to make certain the bags contained everything they needed for a long, uncomfortable hike.

- Water
- Shelter
- Fire
- Food
- Signaling/Communication
- Medical/ Hygiene
- Personal Safety

She washed and dried both Sawyer minis, leaving them to drain beside the sink. She broke her own rule and put two sealed water bottles in each bag. The rain ponchos and bivvy bags were already in the backpacks, just as they should be, and her own pack carried a small, two-person tent.

Each backpack had lighters, and she shoved another one in each of her blue jeans pockets. A flint-and-steel firestarter on a cord went around her neck to be tucked into her t-shirt. The waterproof matches were downstairs, and she wasn't going down there for any money. Lighters and firesteel would have to be enough to satisfy the potential need for fire.

There were already a couple of freeze-dried meals in each bag. From the pantry, she added packets of peanut M&Ms – always her favorite "survival" food due to the fat, carb, and protein mix it offered. She separated the trail mix, bursting with nuts, pumpkin seeds, raisins, and other dried fruits, into individual packets. Finally, she threw in some sticks of jerky. It was only five miles, and they could supplement with foraged items if they got hungry beyond what they carried.

The bags also contained two pairs of extra socks for each of them.

Her cell phone, useless as it was, was completely charged up, and a backup charger went into her bag. Maybe at some high point along the trail, they'd find service. Small, unbreakable mirrors were optimistically included to summon help.

A quick inventory of their IFAKs (individual first-aid kits) confirmed that each was fully stocked with a tourniquet, an Israeli bandage for heavy bleeding, clotting powder, bandages for wrapping a wound, a folding splint, and Band-Aids for blisters. Kate added a bottle of Motrin from her medicine cabinet, along with some allergy pills, Imodium, and Pepto Bismol.

Finally, she strapped her large knife to her waist and tucked the Glock in a holster located at her front right. If she needed it, she'd need it fast. She pulled back the slide and peeked inside. Generally, she didn't keep a round chambered, but today was no ordinary day. She grabbed a neck knife on a piece of camo-patterned paracord and put it on, tucking it into her t-shirt. She took all three extra magazines from a drawer in the short hallway, placing 2 in her bag and 1 in the carrier on her belt.

The bags were ready. While Ariel slumbered on, Kate took a sharp kitchen knife and a cutting board to dice up the wild onions she'd collected yesterday and a bell pepper they'd brought with them. As they sizzled in the pan, she whipped six eggs into a froth with a whisk. Once the eggs had been poured into the pan, she put on the lid to let things cook thoroughly. After a quick stir, cheese from the refrigerator was added to the skillet. Four soft tortillas lay on the cutting board, and she retrieved a bottle of hot sauce.

Ariel stretched and yawned loudly from the sofa, awakened by the aroma of cooking peppers and onions.

Kate smiled and instructed briskly, "Go brush your teeth and your hair, then get dressed for hiking – we're going as soon as you're ready."

Barefoot, her daughter shuffled off to the bathroom, still yawning and shaking off the last vestiges of sleep.

Expertly, Kate filled each tortilla with the scrambled egg mixture and topped them with the appropriate amount of hot sauce. As delicious as the food smelled, Kate was far too uneasy to be hungry.

The parchment paper in the bottom drawer would work to wrap the burritos, and the aluminum foil would keep them warm for a bit longer. She placed the fragrant food into a metal canister she kept expressly to keep food smells inside.

When Ariel reappeared, her wild halo of dark hair had been tamed into two braids, and she had donned her socks and boots. Kate handed her a water-resistant jacket from the hook by the door.

"Coats in September?" Ariel inquired, lifting an arched brow.

"You never know if we might need them."

Kate handed Ariel her pack and a canister of bear spray with a carabiner to clip to her belt loop. She donned the same and began to move the hoosier cabinet that barricaded the kitchen door.

Ariel gasped, "Oh, we almost forgot our bear bells!"

She turned to retrieve them, but Kate stopped her.

"I think we should make as little noise as possible this time."

Ariel froze for a moment, then nodded, squaring her shoulders with determination.

"We're off like a dirty shirt," Kate said.

"Off like a light switch," Ariel replied dutifully.

"Off like a bucket of shrimp in the sun."

"Off like a sweaty sock."

"Off like a.....darn it, you got me," Kate forced a giggle, and Ariel attempted a weak smile.

With that, they were out the back door and ready to begin their journey.

There were a few different ways to get to Mr. Slocum's house, and Kate had all of them memorized for just such an occasion.

"I don't think we should walk down to the road. We'll be too visible. I know we're probably being silly, but..." she shrugged. "I also don't want to take the direct trail."

Ariel suggested, "How about the creek path?"

Kate thought for a moment – there were open areas around the creek, but it was more than a mile from the road and a very roundabout route to the neighbor's place. They wouldn't be seen unless someone was explicitly following them.

"Good idea."

Together, they strode down the hill in silence. The pine needles were still damp from last night's deluge, but their hiking boots had sturdy grips on the bottom. It was a quick walk to the creek and the path beside it.

The real problem was the mud. They trudged through it, but each step was laborious and required far more effort than usual. The squelching sound of their boots sounded as loud as a trumpet, making Kate cringe at their complete and utter lack of stealth. It couldn't be helped, though. If someone had invented a stealthy way to walk through mud, they certainly hadn't taught any of the survival courses Kate had attended.

Wordlessly, Kate handed Ariel one of the breakfast burritos she had wrapped for the hike. The girl gratefully unwrapped it and took a huge bite. Kate took out her own burrito and took a slightly more reserved bite. The savory cheese, well-spiced eggs, and hot sauce had melded into a delicious combination, and neither talked until they finished the first of their breakfast burritos.

"If everything goes well, we should be there in a couple of hours," Kate said, wrapping her foil and waxed paper into a tight ball. She pulled a small folding spade out of her backpack and dug a hole for the wrappers. They couldn't afford to attract bears by packing it out like they usually did.

Ariel followed suit, tossing her own trash into the hole. She dug around for hand sanitizer to take the smell off her hands as Kate covered up the remnants from their breakfast.

Ariel offered her mother a squirt of hand sanitizer. "I'm sure it'll go like clockwork."

"Easy as pie," Kate responded as she rubbed the scented gel onto her hands.

"A piece of cake."

"Child's play."

"Like a walk in the park."

"Like taking candy from a baby."

"Like falling off a log." They both burst into laughter.

"No falling," said Ariel through her giggles. "We have enough problems."

The tension was broken for the moment, and they hiked on, detouring slightly to avoid the worst of the muddy patches that would suck at their boots. *Things seemed to be going smoothly*, thought Kate, feeling a little silly. *I was overreacting.*

Ariel stepped off the path for a moment of privacy, and Kate scanned the area, looking for anything that seemed out of place. Aside from the path carved along the mountain's base, the wooded area looked untouched by humans for centuries.

Kate took her turn behind the bushes, and they set off again, beginning to relax into the meditative calm of the damp forest. The scent of wet pine trees wafted down, enveloping them in the pleasant, clean aroma of a mountain glade after a rainstorm.

Even though the only sounds were their footsteps, crunching and squelching as they marched on, and the rushing waters of the creek,

Suddenly, Kate felt edgy. She had the creepy feeling of being watched, even though she could see no pursuers when she looked behind them.

The path had become even more muddy and slippery. The creek was up due to last night's rainstorm. The hike was more treacherous than normal, and even though they knew the trail well, both concentrated on stepping carefully.

It may have been that concentration that kept them from hearing the threat. Or perhaps the threat was moving through the woods like a ninja. Either way, they went around a bend and started up the next hill when...there it was.

In the middle of the path, in a place where it couldn't be an accident.

A wilted bouquet of sunflowers lay there, its stems wrapped in paper from a florist.

Kate stopped so suddenly that Ariel bumped into her. The giggle was cut short when she saw why her mother had halted.

Ariel froze. The fear that had recently subsided assailed her again, filling her mind, making her incapable of thought.

Kate's mind raced, searching frantically for a logical reason those particular flowers would be on this particular path at this particular time.

There was only one reason.

The memories came rushing back so quickly that Kate felt dizzy.

Chapter 6

Kate felt the earth tilt beneath her, a sudden vertigo sweeping through her as she fought to steady herself.

The dying sunflowers had dropped petals across the path, scattered patches of bruised yellow against the dirt.

...

They had met Logan at a screening of a film about soil in their neighborhood. A local gardening group was showing it in the old vintage theater, and then–11-year-old Ariel had been dragged along as an unwilling companion.

They were hovering over a table with free seed packets, trying to choose, when Kate felt eyes on her. She looked up and saw a handsome man staring at her. She dropped her gaze quickly, peeking through her lashes despite herself.

He was tall, dark-haired, with eyes a shocking blue against his tan face. A perpetual hint of a smile tugged at his mouth and eyes, like he was holding back a private joke. His wavy hair looked silky, and he pushed it off his forehead in an adorably boyish way.

She was surprised when he walked over and introduced himself, asking if he could sit with them since he was new to the area. Afterward, they'd exchanged numbers, though Kate assumed it was courtesy. To her shock, the next morning, Logan texted asking her out to dinner. She eagerly agreed.

He showed up with a huge bouquet of sunflowers.

"How did you know they were my favorite?" Kate asked, delighted.

"You look sunny, so I thought you'd like them," he said with a charming wink.

That date was the first of many. Kate found herself swept away before she realized she was moving. Logan was kind, helpful around the apartment, patient with Ariel's math homework. He brought thoughtful gifts "just because." He was generous, attentive, affectionate—and soon, they both adored him. He spoke casually about their future, about the three of them as "a family."

He became part of their routine with unsettling ease, stopping by daily, picking Ariel up from school, even having a key to start dinner if he was off work early.

There had been flashes of temper. Little bursts—quick, sharp, and immediately smoothed over. A flicker of jealousy, a tense moment. He'd tamp them down so quickly Kate doubted what she'd seen. Everyone got annoyed sometimes, she reasoned.

Then everything collapsed.

...

In the present, Ariel tugged on her arm, saying something Kate couldn't process. Her daughter's voice sounded muffled, foreign.

...

Kate had volunteered to chaperone Ariel's class trip: museums, sightseeing, two nights in a hotel. Logan offered to come. She declined—she'd be rooming with four preteen girls. He sulked. Complained. Pouted. Behavior she'd never seen from him. She told herself it was a fluke.

It wasn't.

During the trip, he bombarded her with calls and texts. She explained she needed to focus on the kids. When she turned her phone off out of desperation, he grew more irrational, accusing her of meeting someone else. She tried to calm him with photos of their activities, but nothing soothed him. The ping of her phone became a trigger—each message tightening the coil in her gut.

Finally, she stopped responding. She knew it would enrage him, but she couldn't keep feeding the cycle.

...

A roar filled her ears—the creek, or the memory, or both—as the present slipped away again.

Ariel kept asking what was wrong. Kate forced a smile she didn't feel and claimed she was tired. On the bus ride home, all she could think about was how to break up with Logan without igniting his temper. She rehearsed conversations, mentally drafting speeches that all fell apart. By the time they pulled into the school parking lot, nausea churned in her stomach.

They picked up the Jeep and grabbed a pizza to stall the inevitable return home. But eventually she had to face it.

Kate trudged up the apartment stairs while Ariel bounded ahead. She paused at the door, listening. Silence. Relief washed through her. Logan hated quiet—he always had music or a podcast going.

She unlocked the door.

The apartment was bursting with sunflowers. Every surface held a bouquet in whatever containers he could find. A note lay on the counter.

"I'm sorry. I just missed you so much."

What once would've seemed romantic now felt suffocating, like a room with no oxygen.

She became wary. She pulled back. And Logan surged forward. He alternated between jealous paranoia and overwhelming affection.

Arguments bloomed where there had never been any, including between Kate and Ariel. And every time, Logan was there, stirring the pot. Divide and conquer.

Kate started hiding her laptop and phone, terrified he'd misinterpret a text or email. She lived in *a perpetual state of bracing: for his anger, for his hurt, for the next imagined offense. When she told her best friend she was deleting their texts constantly, her friend replied, "If you feel the need to do that, you know there's a huge problem, right?"*

That was the moment the blinders came off.

She broke up with him.

To her surprise, he took it calmly. He understood, he said. He knew he'd come on too strong. He asked if he could still see Ariel; Kate told him a clean break was best. When she wouldn't reconsider, he quietly packed his things and left his key on the counter.

She was stunned and relieved that he had taken the breakup so well.

...

"Mom? MOM!" Ariel's hands shook her arm, pulling her back into her body.

Kate jolted, shuddering as she surfaced from the memory.

She and Ariel stood frozen on the trail, staring at the sunflowers like they were a nest of venomous snakes lying in wait.

"You stay right with me. Do you understand?" Kate hissed.

Ariel nodded, wide-eyed.

Kate ran through her options. Three paths, none of them good:

Go back to the cabin.

Walk past the flowers.

Or vanish into the woods.

She didn't know how Logan could be out of prison, but she knew what those flowers meant. No one else would haul city sunflowers up a mountain trail.

A hysterical scrap of a current social media debate flickered across her mind. *Would you rather be trapped in the woods with a bear or a man?*—and a wild giggle tried to claw its way out of her throat.

She swallowed it.

She would rather face a thousand bears than the man who had haunted their lives.

She made her decision. They needed to disappear off the path.

Both she and Ariel were experienced hikers. They knew this mountain, its terrain, its shortcuts, its pitfalls.

Kate scanned the trees, choosing a direction that offered immediate cover.

Then she stepped off the trail, and Ariel followed close enough that Kate could feel her breath on her back.

Chapter 7

A dozen conflicting ideas slamdanced in her head as Kate tried to figure out what to do. Thoughts collided and tangled, none of them fully forming before another crashed into challenge it. But through the mental noise, a single, steady voice rose – the echo of an instructor from her escape-and-evasion course, calm as polished stone.

No plan survives first contact with the enemy...

Go where the enemy will not go...

Do not take the easiest path...

Leave no traces...

The words anchored her. She rolled her shoulders back, quietly exhaled, and led Ariel off the trail into the rocky, shadowed terrain of the deeper forest.

Kate decided their best route was to backtrack toward Mr. Slocum's place, but not directly—not on any predictable line of travel. She would angle around the mountain in a wide loop, avoiding the main path entirely. If Logan was tracking them—and she had absolutely no doubt that he was—she needed to move like prey that refused to behave.

She felt bile rising, the acidic burn tightening her throat. She willed it down. Ariel needed her steady, not unraveling. She feared, deep in her bones, that she could be making everything worse by moving, by walking them straight into a dangerous game of hide-and-seek she never agreed to play.

But standing still would get them killed.

Ariel followed without complaint, though the girl's tears glimmered in the fragments of light filtering through the canopy. They slid silently down her cheeks, catching on her braids. Every now and then, Ariel sniffed quickly, as if embarrassed by the sound.

The sight hardened something inside Kate. Fear twisted into a cold, controlled, surgical rage.

How dare he? How dare Logan reach into their sanctuary, their mountain, their one place of safety, and poison it?

Kate vowed, quietly but fiercely, that she would die before letting him lay a single finger on Ariel.

The forest floor, still slick from last night's downpour, made the trek a battle. Mud sucked at their boots and turned the steeper slopes into treacherous slides. They both slipped repeatedly, catching themselves on rocks and saplings, hands and legs smeared with wet earth. *So much for not leaving a trail*, Kate thought with a frown.

Cold sludge soaked into the fabric of their jeans, but they pushed forward anyway. They had no other choice.

Finally, they reached a downed tree, its trunk mossy and solid—the perfect height for resting. Kate tapped it twice, a silent signal. Ariel sank onto it gratefully, her shoulders drooping with exhaustion and fear. She shrugged off her backpack and unscrewed her water bottle with trembling fingers.

They drank deeply, pausing long enough for their breathing to settle into something quiet and sustainable. Their whispers barely stirred the air.

"Mom..." Ariel wiped her eyes with the back of her hand. "How is Logan here? Isn't he supposed to be in prison for six more years?"

"I thought so, but apparently he's not," Kate whispered. She reached out to pluck a twig from one of Ariel's braids, smoothing it gently. The familiar motion steadied her. "*Why* doesn't matter. What matters is how we avoid him."

Ariel nodded slowly, her lips pressed tight. Kate touched her own hip, confirming the presence of her pistol. Then she dug into her backpack and slid a fresh magazine into her front pocket. Odds were low she'd need it—but these days, odds didn't appear to mean a damn thing.

"Mom... next time we go on vacation, can we just go to the beach?" Ariel quipped in a murmur.

The smallest, strangest bubble of laughter escaped both of them, breaking some of the tension they had been carrying. They tucked their water away and stood again.

"We've trained for this," Kate reminded her, though her voice wavered just enough that she hoped Ariel didn't catch it. "Remember the course in Colorado? This is just the real version of that." Their instructor had taught them to vanish into the forest, to move like wind and shadow, to think in circles instead of lines.

Kate always had a strong sense of direction. Her father used to jokingly call her "Magellan." Even without a trail, she trusted herself to navigate. They pressed upward, stepping carefully between slick roots and hidden holes.

Since speaking could travel farther in the forest than footsteps, Kate let her mind slip into her familiar ritual—a tally of everything she had trained herself to become. A list she recited whenever she felt the old, paralyzing Kate tugging at her ankles.

She wasn't the girl who told the cops what happened while shaking so hard she could barely sign the statement.

She wasn't the woman who once flinched at the sound of a phone vibrating.

She wasn't helpless.

She could build a shelter from nothing.

Shoot with accuracy under pressure.

Wield a recurve longbow with surprising precision.

Defend herself with knives.

Traverse unfamiliar terrain after days of exhaustion.

Outrun and outsmart an opponent who underestimated her.

Forage for food.

Move with stealth.

Stay alive.

Ariel had learned right beside her with every course that allowed her presence. Kate knew without question that her daughter was capable of far more than she realized. The only thing that concerned her was whether panic would smother the girl's training.

Kate prayed that adrenaline would sharpen Ariel rather than drown her.

She thought of the Krav Maga drills with the strobe lights and bone-rattling heavy metal music. The disorientation training. The stress inoculation. The instructors yelling inches from their faces. She hoped it all lived in Ariel's muscles the way it did in hers.

Everything Kate had built—the strength, the discipline, the transformation—felt like a protective shell she desperately hoped wouldn't crack today.

She tried not to think about those years. But the past was stubborn. It crept in at the edges, memories scratching their way back to the surface. She exhaled through them, calling on therapy techniques.

Stay in the present. Anchor. Focus. Choose clarity over fear.

So focused was she on her breathing that she nearly jumped when Ariel grabbed her wrist.

Ahead, tucked deep between thick spruces, nearly invisible unless you were looking for it, was a campsite.

Kate's stomach dropped.

She grabbed Ariel's shirt and pulled her behind a large boulder and a fallen log. They pressed into the shadows, barely daring to inhale.

The tent was a drab forest green—army surplus, probably. Cigarette smoke clung to the clearing, threading between the pines. A food bag hung from a high branch, clean and recently tied. The ground around the tent was disturbed, but not by weather—by footsteps.

This wasn't an old campsite.

Someone was living here.

Someone without a campfire.

Someone trying not to be seen.

Someone who knew how to hide.

Her mind tried to offer her a lifeline—maybe a backpacker, maybe a lost wanderer, maybe a hobo—but her instincts rejected it immediately.

This was deliberate. Intentional. Recent.

Her pulse thudded in her ears hard enough to blur her vision. Thoughts tumbled, collided, twisted. She couldn't believe she went off the trail and nearly walked right into somebody's camp.

Backtrack?

Circle wide around?

Freeze until the owner returned and hope he wasn't a threat?

Return to the cabin and barricade again?

But where was Logan?

If this was his camp, and she knew, with sick certainty, that it was, then where was he right now? Ahead of them? Behind them? Watching them?

How had she let him outmaneuver her? How had she been so careful and still walked her child into danger?

She forced herself to stop spiraling. She needed logic. Options. She needed—

A sound cut through the forest.

Footfalls.

Crunching leaves. Slow. Heavy. Deliberate.

Ariel's fingers tightened on Kate's flannel.

Kate surged forward, instinct overriding thought, placing herself between the sound and her daughter.

She drew her Glock in one smooth motion, raising it toward the unseen movement, index finger along the frame, ready to move to the trigger in a millisecond.

Her heart hammered, but her grip stayed steady.

Please be a bear, she prayed. *Please be anything but him.*

Chapter 8

It felt difficult to breathe. Kate struggled to inhale fully, as if her lungs were packed with wool. Panic sat on her chest like a living thing, compressing, suffocating, stealing the space where oxygen should have been.

Thinking about walking back through the forest made it worse.

Nightmarish memories bled into the edges of her vision, staggering her. The shadows between trees flickered with the shapes of things she prayed she would never see again. She blinked hard, tried to drag herself back to the present—the mud, the wet leaves, the cold air scraping at her throat—but her mind kept slipping.

...

After Logan left—after she finally told him no more, no second chances, no more keys to her life—Kate reveled in the sudden, blessed silence of her apartment. The atmosphere changed so abruptly that it felt like stepping into clean air after weeks of smog.

She could breathe again. Really breathe.

The walls seemed brighter without him in them. The air felt lighter. She let herself believe that she and Ariel would heal quickly now that the source of their tension had been removed. Logan had been infiltrating their bond in subtle, insidious ways—comments dropped strategically, jealous insinuations, attempts to position himself between them. But Kate knew her daughter and knew their connection. With him gone, they would recalibrate.

She hadn't been sleeping well for months. The constant vigilance, the way she listened for the door, the anxiety of never knowing what version of Logan she'd get...it had all worn her down.

So she decided to take a nap.

A simple thing. Ordinary. Safe.

She curled onto her bed, savoring the feeling of peace. She hadn't realized how heavy the emotional weight had become until its absence made her feel almost floaty, untethered. Her last thought before drifting off was something close to gratitude.

She slid into the deepest sleep she'd felt in ages...

...until consciousness slammed into her like a fist.

Kate jolted awake, but she couldn't move. A crushing weight pinned her to the mattress. For one disoriented second, she thought she was caught in sleep paralysis.

Then something pressed across her neck—hard, unyielding—forcing her face deeper into the sheets.

Air exploded out of her lungs. She tried to pull in another breath, but the sheets sucked into her nostrils, blocking everything. *The more she inhaled, the more the fabric sealed against her skin. Panic flickered into full wildfire.*

She was suffocating. Someone was suffocating her.

Her fingers clawed weakly at the bed. Her legs kicked. The edges of her vision blurred gray.

Then a voice—low, familiar, dripping with venom—growled into her ear.

"Stop. Fighting."

Her entire body froze.

Logan.

The sound of his voice detonated something inside her, a visceral terror that lived in her bones. Her mind shrieked, No, no, no—this can't be real, but her body already knew it was true.

He eased the pressure only enough for her to drag in a single, ragged breath. Tears stung instantly, hot and blinding.

"We were a family," he whispered, his voice cracking like something fractured inside him.

She didn't move. Didn't speak. She knew too well that any wrong word could be gasoline on a fire.

"We were a family," he repeated, louder now, anger blooming beneath his words. "And you destroyed it. What really happened on that field trip? Who did you see?" His accusations escalated rapidly—wild, snarling leaps of paranoia.

Kate stayed petrified, tears soaking into the sheets beneath her face.

"Why would you ruin everything?" he demanded. "We were a family. If you didn't want me, fine. But why ruin it for Ari? She loved me. I loved her. She was like my own daughter."

A surge of hate pulsed through him; she felt it in the tension of his body, the shift of his weight.

Then, abruptly, the pressure lifted.

For a fragile, suspended heartbeat, she thought he was getting off her.

Relief flared.

Until she felt hands at her waistband.

No.

No no no.

He yanked her sweatpants down in one brutal motion. Kate twisted, panic exploding into ferocity, but he grabbed a fistful of her hair and slammed her face into the mattress again.

She couldn't breathe. Couldn't scream. Couldn't pull enough air to fight. The sheets filled her nose and mouth, choking her. She gagged and coughed, body convulsing.

Her vision cracked like glass. The room stretched and warped, collapsing at the corners.

She made a noise—a high, broken sound—but it wasn't loud enough to draw attention to her plight. Not nearly enough.

Her limbs turned weak and numb. Her fingers clawed desperately at the sheets, at the mattress, at anything.

A roaring filled her ears. A buzzing. A pressure.

Then—

Nothing.

...

She tried to shake the memory away, to force herself back into the forest and the immediate danger at hand. But the memory didn't ask permission—it replayed itself, unspooling inside her mind with the clarity of a waking nightmare.

...

Consciousness seeped back into her body that day like a tide returning slowly, reluctantly.

Everything hurt.

Her head pulsed with a deep ache. Her throat felt scraped raw. Her ribs protested with each shallow breath. But she lay still, too terrified to move, listening.

Was he still here?

Silence.

Not safety. Just...silence.

She tested a toe. A finger. Her legs. They responded, though everything felt bruised, wrong, foreign. She rolled onto her side, and a sharp, sudden pain flared through her hips.

Her sweatpants were gone.

They lay crumpled in the corner like discarded evidence.

Blood stained the sheets.

But she was alive.

Somehow.

A single breath escaped her—thin and shaking. Then another.

Ariel.

The thought ripped through her like a grenade had detonated.

Kate lurched upright, the panic so immediate it left her dizzy. She staggered out of the bedroom, frantically scanning the floor.

Her nightstand was empty.

Her phone—gone.

She dropped to her knees, searching under the bed, under the dresser, behind the door. Nothing.

She began to frantically search the house, still naked from the waist down.

Then she found it.

Shattered pieces of her phone lay strewn across the kitchen tile, stomped into ruin.

Her blood went cold.

No landline. No neighbors in the small building were home during the day. There was no way to call anyone.

And no way to know where Logan had gone.

"Ariel." Her voice was a broken whisper.

She rushed back into the bedroom, pulling on her sweatpants even as she moved toward the kitchen again. Her hands shook so hard she fumbled twice before closing her waistband.

Keys. She needed her keys.

She snatched them from the counter with trembling fingers and bolted out the door barefoot. She didn't even close it behind her. She flew down the stairs, lungs burning, legs shaking, her body screaming from the trauma, but her mind screaming louder.

She didn't obey traffic laws. Lights were suggestions. Lanes were irrelevant. Every second mattered.

"Let Ariel be okay, let Ariel be okay, let Ariel be okay—"

The mantra spilled out in a frantic loop as she sped through intersections, cut around cars, and screeched into the school parking lot so fast the Jeep hopped the curb.

She ran to the front entrance, slamming her fist against the buzzer.

"Please—please—please—"

The intercom crackled.

"This is Janice Jones. May I help—"

"Ariel!" Kate screamed. "ARIEL!"

"Mrs. Lindsey?" Janice, the school secretary, sounded startled, alarmed.

Kate's breath came in sharp, jagged bursts. "Where is my daughter?"

Footsteps moved quickly inside. Kate barely registered them. Her gaze flicked upward toward the security camera, catching sight of herself in the reflection: hair wild, shirt torn, mascara smeared, bruises already blooming beneath her skin.

She saw a woman she barely recognized.

Janice appeared behind the glass, and her face changed instantly.

"Mrs. Lindsey...what happened?"

Kate's words splintered into sobs. "Did he take her? Did he take my baby?"

"Who? Logan?" Janice asked, frowning. "He just picked her up. He said she had a dental appointment. He was on the approved list—"

Kate collapsed.

Her knees hit the concrete, then her hands, then she vomited, body heaving uncontrollably. Her entire world narrowed into a single, echoing thought:

He has my baby. She's only 10 years old, and my baby is alone with an unpredictable monster.

...

A rustling in the underbrush snapped Kate back into the present with vicious clarity.

Her hands trembled uncontrollably. Her breath came too fast, too shallow.

But she forced her mind still.

Forced her lungs steady.

Forced herself back into the calm she had built over three long years. They had to move.

She closed her eyes for one heartbeat, centering herself.

Never again, she swore. *He will not hurt us.*

Not me.

Not my daughter.

Not ever.

Chapter 9

Taking a deep breath, Kate knew they had to move. The breath didn't feel like enough – it snagged halfway down – but it was all she had. She nudged Ariel, and they both took a quiet step back toward the safe depths of the forest, away from the trail that now felt exposed and wrong.

They didn't speak. Their silence was deliberate, tactical. They took great care to avoid stepping on twigs that would snap underfoot or leaves that would crunch. Every step was a calculation: weight on the ball of the foot, roll to the heel, check the ground before shifting. Kate pulled the pistol from her holster and kept it in her hand, muzzle pointed safely toward the ground just like she'd practiced a hundred times in training. She heard Ariel's quick intake of breath when she saw the gun in her mother's hand, but she ignored it, leading the way deeper into the maze of trees.

The forest closed around them, damp and shadowed. The smell of wet earth and pine needles wrapped around them, thick as a blanket. Somewhere far off, the creek muttered over rocks, but up here every tiny sound felt magnified – a distant birdcall, the rustle of a squirrel, the whisper of leaves under their boots.

"Mom."

Ariel said the word in a whimper, like a plea, like a tiny thread thrown desperately toward her.

Kate turned with her fingers to her lips to shush Ariel. She expected to see her daughter right where she'd left her, eyes wide, scared but free.

She froze when she saw her.

Adrenaline flooded her body, with nowhere to go. It was like being plugged into a live wire. Her vision blurred for a moment—was it from panic? denial? rage?—and she had to blink her eyes and take a deep breath to clear them.

Ariel was being embraced by the worst mistake she had ever made.

Logan's arm was around her, casual and possessive in one motion, like it belonged there. Ariel's thin shoulders were rigid under his grip. Her braids brushed his chest. They looked, at a glance, like a father and daughter on a hike. As long as you didn't look too carefully at Ariel's widened eyes or the stiff way she stood, clearly terrified.

Any way that Kate could think of to fight put her baby at risk.

Every scenario flashed through her mind in fast-forward.

Lunge, and he could use Ariel as a shield.

Shoot, and she could hit the wrong body.

Run, and he'd drag Ariel away with him.

Kate felt completely helpless as her mind raced for a solution but found none. The forest tilted sideways, leaving her off balance, like the ground itself was trying to throw her.

His dark hair was buzzed into a short cap on his head, instead of silky waves that had given him a boyish look. The haircut made his cheekbones look sharper, his face more angular. He was thinner than before, but it was the type of thinness that suggested wiry speed and strength. His face looked harder, somehow, with a different set to his jaw. Prison had carved the softness out of him.

The eyes she used to fondly think of as cerulean blue now seemed like the specific shade that appeared, snapping and painfully hot, when you lit a gas stove.

"Hi, ladies," Logan grinned darkly at them, teeth so white and prominent that Kate was reminded of the wolf in Grandma's bed, trying to fool Little Red Riding Hood into thinking he was harmless. "Great day for a hike, isn't it?"

His voice sounded almost cheerful, almost normal, and that made it worse. The false brightness scraped along her nerves like sandpaper.

Ariel fired back to life, preparing to struggle. Kate saw the impulse in her eyes, the way her muscles tensed, the tiny jerk of her shoulders as she got ready to wrench away. She was subdued when Kate glanced in warning at her, and she halted her fight before it began. Kate could see her daughter trembling, the fine quiver in her jaw, the way her knees knocked together, but she couldn't think about that now.

If she let herself really see the terror written all over her daughter, she'd break down and never get back up.

She didn't know how...

She didn't know when...

But she would get her chance, and Logan was going to find out that she wasn't the same victim who had cried on the witness stand explaining what he'd done to her and to Ariel. She could still feel the ghost of that courtroom under her skin – the hard wooden chair, the stale air, his eyes on her, looking slightly amused, as she spoke.

That woman had been afraid.

This one was furious.

"Fancy meeting you here," she greeted him with false calmness and courtesy.

Her voice didn't shake. She clung to that.

"Yeah. Fancy that."

The smile Logan flashed did not reach his eyes, and Kate could feel the rage emanating from him. It rolled off him in waves, hot and toxic. "I love family hiking trips. Coming out here with my family was one of my favorite memories over the past three years, three months, and six days."

He said the time down to the day. Of course he did. Of course, he'd been counting.

"We are not your family, Logan. Any chance of that ended when you attacked me and kidnapped my daughter."

The words came out flat and controlled, but inside, she was shaking.

Logan pulled Ariel in closer to him. Her eyes looked panicked, and Kate couldn't stare into them and keep her cool, so she met Logan's eyes instead.

He wanted the reaction, wanted the plea.

She refused to give it to him.

"I was like a father to this girl." His voice broke when he said the words. He looked down at Ariel, who barely made it to his shoulder. "I love you, Ari. I love you."

As he used his free hand to lift her chin and meet her eyes, Ariel closed them shut tightly and refused. Tears escaped, making trails down her lightly freckled cheeks. The sight made Kate's chest ache, but she couldn't move. Not yet. He gave a grim chuckle. "It's okay, honey. I know your mother has been telling you lies about me.

"There's a name for that, you know." He turned his attention back to Kate. "Parental alienation."

"You aren't Ariel's parent, and you alienated yourself when you kidnapped her," Kate retorted.

Her voice was cool. Detached. It was the only way to keep from screaming.

"Put the gun down, Kate," he ordered. "We both know you aren't going to use it."

He was right about one thing: with Ariel in his grip, she couldn't. Not yet.

Carefully...

Regretfully...

Hesitantly...

Kate laid the Glock down on the ground. She felt the loss immediately—the weight gone, the control gone. Her palm felt strangely naked without the familiar heft of the weapon.

It's too risky to take a shot with Ariel in between them, she told herself. She heard the voice of a previous instructor in her head. "You have to wait for the right moment. Don't take your chance too early, while your opponent is alert and waiting for it. Bide your time."

Bide your time, bide your time, bide your time, she chanted mentally, breathing slowly, calming herself. Slow inhale. Long exhale. Don't let him see you shake.

"Now, kick it over here to me."

Kate indulged in a small rebellion by kicking the firearm off the trail into a pile of leaves, instead of directly at his feet. Logan's eyes flashed with something terrifying for a moment, a flash of the temper she knew all too well. He caught himself, chuckled, and kept his hold on Ariel as he moved over to get the gun and stick it in his own waistband.

"Let's go back and have some lunch. I'm starving," said Logan, as though it was a normal Sunday afternoon frolic in the woods.

Kate stared at him, mouth open, like he had suggested they ride elephants or fly on a magic carpet to return to the cabin. Lunch. Like they were just...out here making memories.

He turned, arm still around Ariel, and began to stride toward the path back to the cabin. His hold on her was firm enough to guide, loose enough to pretend it was affection.

Kate had no choice but to follow.

Bide your time.

Bide your time.

She gave herself a mental shake. She'd have to play along for now. There were no good options, only less catastrophic ones.

"I'll make us some soup and sandwiches," Kate said agreeably as she followed. If Logan was crazy enough to believe they still had a chance at being a family, she was determined to lull him into thinking she was under his spell again. She could fake domesticity. She'd done it before. She'd do it again, only this time with an exit plan.

It enraged her to think that she had gone from competent survivalist to captive in the space of a moment. All because she had reacted too slowly. All because she hadn't seen him in time.

Her anger fueled her on the long, wordless walk back to the cabin. She counted steps. Counted breaths.

Counted seconds until the moment she could break him. The forest that had felt like a sanctuary now felt like a mouth closing around them.

By the time they had reached the cabin, the sun was much lower in the western sky. Kate estimated it was around five o'clock. Her stomach growled as she thought about food. It seemed so weird that she could still feel hungry under these circumstances, but even if she hadn't been, she'd have forced some nourishment into herself. She needed protein, calories, and a clear head. You couldn't fight or think straight on an empty tank.

Once inside the cabin, Logan pulled a handful of zip ties from his pocket and restrained them, hands behind their backs, to two of the kitchen chairs that had been piled against the basement door. The plastic bit into her skin with every movement. He chuckled at her desperate fortifications, which infuriated Kate anew. All that planning, all that barricading—and he'd walked right around it.

Discreetly, she tugged at the ziptie that held her wrists together, only to find it so snug it nearly cut the skin as she tried to separate her hands. All the ways she knew of getting out of zipties were rendered obsolete by the fact that she was also fastened to the chair, and she couldn't get her arms in front of her. She mentally ran through every trick she'd learned—wriggling, using friction, leveraging against the knee—but none of them worked from this angle.

Efficiently, he collected the sharp knives from the kitchen, the bear spray from their backpacks, and everything else that they might use to fight back against him. It almost felt like he'd read her mind as she desperately catalogued makeshift weapons. Every time she thought, *We could use that*, he picked it up. Her heart sank further with each item he gathered.

It was like watching her options get erased one by one.

His collection of potential weaponry filled his arms. Kate allowed herself a small, internal chuckle. He thought she was dangerous.

Oh, she was. And she didn't need a marble rolling pin or kitchen knife to prove it.

He left briefly to hide the items like they were contraband, giving Kate and Ariel a moment together. The cabin felt strangely hollow without the clank of metal and scrape of wood, the absence of potential weapons making the space feel smaller.

"It's going to be okay, Ariel," Kate told her daughter firmly. "We have to wait for our chance. We have to make him think he's won and that we've given up. Can you do that for me?"

"No!" Ariel began to cry, large tears rolling down her cheeks. "I hate him. I don't want to be nice to him."

Kate leaned in, pressing her forehead gently to Ariel's. For one fragile second, they simply breathed together, the rise and fall of their chests syncing like it had so many nights after nightmares. Kate could smell Ariel's shampoo, the faint salt of tears, the lingering scent of woodsmoke from earlier. *This* was her real life. Logan was the intrusion.

Finally, Kate spoke again.

"I know, but it's the only way we're going to get the chance to escape. I want you to keep your boots on at all times, even in bed. We are going to get out of here. Do you understand me? Do not let him scare you and take away all that you've learned since he's been gone. We need to make him feel like he's already won so that we can catch him by surprise."

She could see the shift in Ariel's expression as the words landed—the way fear made a tiny bit of room for grim determination.

Ariel sniffed and nodded. She lifted her chin and clenched her teeth. "Then you're gonna beat him like a redheaded stepchild, right?"

Kate giggled at the old Appalachian turn of phrase. Even now, it punched a tiny hole in the terror. She felt better, knowing that Ariel would play along.

Logan didn't know it yet, but these two familiar faces hid two very different women from those he had known before. He had no idea what he was in for, and that was exactly how Kate liked it.

When he returned to the cabin, he cut the zip ties off both of them. The plastic snapped with a sharp, humiliating sound. He enticed Ariel into a game of dominoes, which she agreed to with a minuscule clench of her jaw that only Kate would notice.

Meanwhile, Kate puttered around the kitchen, the picture of domesticity. She popped open a jar of minestrone she had home-canned, and while it was warming on the stovetop, she made sandwiches with some of the deli meat and cheese she'd brought from the city. She had to saw the sandwiches in half with a table knife since Logan had taken away all of the chef's knives. The blunt blade dragged through the bread, making uneven crumbs scatter across the cutting board.

She moved all the furniture back to its appropriate spot. The heavy job helped her cope with some of the adrenaline coursing through her body with no place to go. Muscles needed something to do. If she didn't move, she'd shake.

She set the table with her cheerful red speckleware and added a cloth napkin to each place setting. By the time that task was complete, the soup had reached a boiling point. She ladled the steaming, fragrant mixture into bowls she had thrifted, which had handles and the old Campbell's logo on them. It looked like the kind of lunch from a commercial. It felt like a scene from a horror movie.

"Lunch," she announced with fake cheer.

"Ariel is stomping me at dominoes!" Logan exclaimed. "You've gotten really good at that game." He gave the girl a fond, paternal look. After a momentary internal battle over her facial expressions, she smiled back wanly. Kate watched the micro-expressions flash across Ariel's face: disgust, fear, calculation, then the thin, brittle smile.

As Kate poured lemonade into Mason jar glasses, they sat at the cheerfully set table. Kate and Ariel sat stiffly, uncomfortably, as they struggled to appear accommodating. Logan sat at the head of the table, leaning back, surveying the room like a king looking out over his dominion. He looked satisfied. That, more than anything, made Kate's stomach turn.

Outwardly, they looked just like the family Logan wanted them to be.

For now.

Chapter 10

The afternoon dragged on at a glacial pace into early evening.

The minutes crawled, stretching longer than they had any right to, each one weighed down by awareness and dread. The light slanted differently through the trees with every passing moment, the day bleeding slowly toward night.

Logan dragged a chair from the kitchen to add to the two already on the porch. The shrill scrape of wood across the floor made Kate's shoulders tense despite her efforts to remain still.

He, Kate, and Ariel sat together on the screened-in porch like some twisted imitation of a family evening. He had pulled a few bottles of beer from his knapsack and tucked them into the fridge before dinner, and now he drank one with lazy, proprietary satisfaction.

He looked comfortable. Settled. As though this were his house and not Kate's.

Outside, fireflies blinked in and out of visibility over the clearing, tiny floating lanterns blissfully unaware of the scene unfolding nearby. Ariel watched them with hollow eyes. Her gaze followed their flickering paths as if she could disappear into that soft, glowing darkness with them.

Kate tracked them, too, but only because she feared that if she let her eyes rest on Logan's face for too long, the crack in her composure would widen into something visible.

Logan sighed contentedly, eyes closed. It was the sound of a man savoring victory and dominion.

"You can't imagine how often I've dreamed about the three of us sitting here just like this."

Kate and Ariel stayed silent. *If you can't say something nice...*

When he opened his eyes, he looked at them with a devotion so misplaced it tightened Kate's stomach. "We can overcome all of this," he said softly. "I forgive you both."

Kate shut her eyes, clenching her back teeth to keep the outrage off her face. The word "forgive" echoed in her skull, sharp and absurd. Forgive? *Forgive?* He was willing to f*orgive* her and Ariel? For surviving him?

She breathed slowly, counting her breaths to control the tremor in her hands. *Bide your time.*

"Ariel, why don't you go brush your teeth and get ready for bed?" Logan suggested.

Kate nodded at Ariel, the nod of a mother trying to communicate Go. Don't argue. Stay safe. Ariel hesitated, then left to brush her teeth.

Kate braced herself. She could feel the tension rising like static. Heaven only knew what this delusional man had planned now that he had her alone. If he had any romantic intentions, he was in for a harsh awakening. There wasn't enough "bide your time" in the world for that.

Logan took another long drink, draining the bottle. He set it aside lazily. Kate rose to get him another, thinking maybe — just maybe — he'd drink himself stupid.

His hand shot out and grabbed her wrist. "It's okay. I'm good for now." His grip was light, almost gentle — and, somehow, that made it worse.

He smiled like this was a perfectly normal evening, like they were still his little household and he hadn't blown their lives to pieces. Kate's thoughts churned, but outwardly she kept herself serene, neutral, and careful.

Ariel returned in sweats and a big t-shirt, her boots still on. Logan smirked at the picture of a rabbit wearing over the ear headphones on the front of her tee. "Give me the boots, Ari."

"My feet are cold," Ariel argued weakly.

"Then put on extra socks. Boots off, now."

Kate kept her voice mild. "It's okay, honey. Just grab the slippers from your room." Kate always had a Plan B cooking. The boots were only a minor setback.

Ariel's mutiny was visible in every line of her body, but she obeyed, stomping back out in her ridiculous brown fuzzy slippers with Yeti heads adorning each foot. Logan laughed at the goofy footwear. "I'm glad you still have the same sense of humor, honey."

Ariel raised one eyebrow but didn't speak.

"Don't go to sleep just yet," Logan added. "Go read your book for a while. I have to make some special arrangements for your sleeping quarters tonight."

Kate resisted the urge to ask what on earth that meant. She let the unease sit there like a stone. Her calm mask stayed fixed, though her stomach had bottomed out.

Ariel flounced into her room. Logan called after her, "Door stays open!"

Ariel flung her bedroom door back with an irritable slam — hitting the wall hard enough to rattle a picture frame. Logan chuckled, as if this were just plain old teenage sass rather than traumatized fury.

He gestured Kate toward the kitchen. They sat on two of the dining chairs, facing one another.

The table felt suddenly too small, the space between them too intimate. Kate resisted the instinct to angle her body away from him, knowing retreat would read as fear.

"I want to trust you," he began, his voice low and raw. "But I can't. Not yet. What you did to me... let's just say prison wasn't a picnic."

Kate's patience snapped like brittle kindling. The restraint she'd been white-knuckling finally splintered. "What I did to *you*?" she hissed. "What about what you did to us? You took my child. You raped me."

Logan looked wistfully out the window, sighing like a disappointed teacher. His voice was soft, hurt, when he spoke. "It wasn't like that. You misinterpreted things.

I was taking Ariel on a father–daughter trip. And you always liked it a little rough, Katie. I just gave you what you wanted."

Kate was rendered speechless. Her mouth fell open before she could stop it. When he reached across the table and gently pushed her jaw shut with one finger, she jerked back, revulsion shuddering through her.

He was more delusional than she'd ever feared — rewriting reality to protect whatever fragile ego kept his rage burning.

"I don't trust you not to overreact again," he went on. "And I need rest. I've been out in those woods for two weeks now, sleeping on the ground." He yawned dramatically, like he'd been kept awake by noisy neighbors rather than stalking them.

Two weeks of watching. Two weeks of waiting.

"So you and Ari are going to sleep in the basement tonight."

Kate forced a flash of annoyance across her face so Logan would think she objected. Inside, relief flickered for the small, unexpected mercy. The basement meant concrete walls and a door between them. The basement meant distance. Distance meant safety. For tonight, at least.

"Tomorrow, you and I will talk things out," Logan went on. "Look at what I've done to get you back. Isn't it obvious I still love you, even after you sent me to prison?"

"Sure," Kate said lightly, with the casual tone of someone agreeing to discuss paint colors, not their own abduction. "We'll talk tomorrow."

He stood and shoved the table away from the basement door. He chuckled at the barricade. "Wow. You two really didn't want company."

Kate delivered the performance of her life.

"We didn't know it was you last night, Logan. We had no idea you'd been released. When the door was open, and the Jeep wouldn't start... we thought it was someone dangerous."

She let her voice tremble – just enough to sound real.

She managed a shaky breath. "I was just trying to keep Ariel safe."

He nodded thoughtfully, buying the story. He loved their fear. He fed on it. It was the only currency he believed in.

Kate followed when he went into Ariel's room, where she was trying her very hardest to disappear into her book.

"I need your mattress," he said.

Ariel froze, blanching, but didn't argue — not after meeting Kate's eyes and seeing approval. Together, they dragged the mattress to the door. Logan shoved it down the stairs, where it thumped heavily onto the concrete.

Kate grabbed quilts from the closet and tossed them down, too. Their colors flashed briefly in the dim stairwell — cheerful, domestic things repurposed for captivity.

Logan flung down four pillows.

"I know how you girls love your pillows," he said with a fond, reminiscent smile that made Kate's skin crawl. "I want you to be comfortable."

She fought to keep her face neutral.

"Now your boots," he said to Kate. "I don't trust either of you not to try running, but I seriously doubt you'd run through the woods barefoot. Just a little lesson I picked up in my former accommodations."

Kate removed her hiking boots slowly, trying to seem resentful that he mistrusted her. She donned her pink fuzzy slippers.

She and Ariel each took a turn in the bathroom, then gathered books—their tiny defense against fear—and met at the basement door.

Logan kissed Ariel on the forehead. "Goodnight, sweetie. Tomorrow we'll play dominoes again."

Ariel endured it without pulling away. The restraint cost her, Kate could see that.

Ariel swallowed hard. "Yeah," she muttered, then clomped down the stairs as aggressively as possible in her Yeti slippers.

Kate went to follow, but Logan's hand clamped around her wrist once more. She turned, ready to fight despite her plans to appear accommodating. His very touch made her practically blind with rage.

"I still love you, Katie," he said intensely, eyes locked on hers.

He leaned forward. Kate braced for a real kiss, stomach twisting — but he kissed her forehead instead.

Kate descended the stairs so fast she nearly tripped. She didn't slow down until her feet touched the concrete of the basement floor. Logan slid the Molly bar back into place. The heavy clunk of it settling in the brackets should have filled her with dread.

Instead, it was blessed relief.

Ariel had already positioned the mattress along the wall and stacked the pillows and quilts into a makeshift bed. She had found one of their small battery lanterns, setting it so the warm glow softened the harsh concrete room.

Kate sank onto the mattress and pulled Ariel into her arms. The girl sobbed, shaking with the terror she had been holding at bay. Kate stroked her hair, murmuring reassurance—but her mind was already racing.

Logan had locked them in the room with all their supplies. Their water, their food, their gear. Their advantage.

He thought the basement was a cage.

Kate saw a staging ground.

Idiot, she thought.

She gave it one night. Let him think he'd broken them. Let him relax. Let him underestimate them.

He always had.

Ariel drifted into exhausted sleep. Her breathing evened out, nice and steady.

Kate lay awake a bit longer, planning, counting supplies, mapping the routes through the forest in her head.

Eventually, even she succumbed to sleep — uneasy but necessary.

The lantern glowed steadily in the darkness, a tiny, stubborn beacon against the night.

Chapter 11

Kate awoke to the sound of the Molly bar being removed and the door to the basement opening. She froze, not daring to exhale, certain that Logan was going to come downstairs. When she heard his footsteps in the kitchen, she let out the breath she had been holding in a long, quiet whoosh.

Upstairs, cups were clinking, cabinets were opening and closing. It was the sound of a man settling in and making himself at home.

She remained still in body, but her brain was racing as she began to plot their escape. She catalogued details reflexively: time of day, direction of light through the basement windows, sounds from above, Ariel's breathing beside her.

She thought back to that course she had taken in Mexico about surviving a kidnapping. The instructor's face surfaced in her memory, stern and unsmiling, weathered by the sun until it looked like old leather.

If you're kidnapped, don't take the first chance to try and escape unless it's completely bulletproof. Your attacker will be watching for that. Initially they'll be alert to your attempts to free yourself. Lull them into complacency by seeming to comply. Wait until their guard drops and then make your escape.

Kate had written those words down in a notebook at the time, underlining them twice. Now, she repeated them silently like a mantra.

She would spend the day making Logan think he'd won and the "family" he so treasured was back together. Part of her rebelled at the thought of being nice to him, but the more logical part won out, knowing it was the best way to cause him to drop his defenses. He was bigger and stronger than them. Their only hope for victory was to be smarter.

He'd made several mistakes already, she mused. He'd locked them in with their survival supplies. He'd put them together so they could plot against him. But worse, for him, he thought they were the same tearful victims he'd left behind in that courtroom when he was sentenced to prison.

That miscalculation would be his undoing, she thought with satisfaction.

She rolled onto her side and watched Ariel's chest rise and fall as she snored softly. She hated to rouse her back into their current situation, but this might be their only chance to speak privately.

Gently, she shook Ariel's shoulder until the girl began to stir.

Kate put her finger to her lips in a "shush" sign. Ariel nodded sleepily. Kate began to whisper the plan to her.

"We have to make Logan think he's won and that we're all 'together' again," she told her daughter.

Ariel's face was instantly mutinous. "I won't be nice to him," she stated, shoulders set stubbornly.

Kate understood that instinct, but strategy demanded a different course.

"Ariel – you *have* to be nice to him. Don't go overboard or he'll know we're lying, but be civil and try to act like you used to act with him before everything went bad. I promise, tonight we will get out, but today we have to play along."

Ariel set her jaw and looked as annoyed as a teenage girl can look – which was pretty darned irritated. Finally, she relented with an aggrieved sigh. "Fine."

"Promise me," Kate urged. They were a family that took promises as seriously as a blood oath.

Ariel rolled her eyes. "I promise. I'll behave."

"I want you to stay away from us as much as possible and read your book. Keep your distance but don't make it look weird, okay?"

Ariel nodded again.

"Now, let's get up and put on a show. I love you."

Reluctantly, Ariel sat up in bed and stretched. "I love you, too, Mom."

And...action! thought Kate as, together, they padded up the wooden stairs in their slippers.

...

While Ariel went to the bathroom, Kate sat down at the kitchen table with Logan. Her voice trembled, and she let it, hoping that it would reinforce his feeling of being in charge. "Logan, please... I can't fight anymore. Let's talk."

She curled her shoulders inward, made herself smaller—something she hadn't done in years. She looked at the floor to keep him from reading the defiance in her eyes.

"It's not that easy to have a casual conversation with the woman who ruined my life, took my family away, and sent me to prison," he replied with a hard set to his jaw. After a pause, he continued in a softer tone. "But I still love you, Katie. I don't know why, but I do."

"I was in the wrong," Kate lied, inwardly grimacing. Her voice broke. "Can you ever forgive me?"

Each word felt like she was swallowing glass.

Logan reached across the table and cupped her cheek with his big, calloused hand. She steeled herself not to flinch and gazed back at him.

"Katie, I missed you."

She busied herself by counting the number of heartbeats it took him to release her face. Five.

"I missed you, too, Logan. I think Ariel's out of the bathroom now." She forced herself not to sprint to the restroom that Ariel had just vacated. The teen had vanished behind her closed bedroom door, just as instructed, Kate noticed approvingly.

Once she took as long as she dared in the bathroom, she returned to the kitchen and poured herself some of the coffee Logan had brewed. She added cream and sugar to her cup and began to make herself busy, tying on an apron and preparing breakfast. The man she had once thought she loved stared at her with yearning that made her skin prickle in the most unpleasant way possible.

She fell into the soothing routine of making breakfast. Bacon sizzled while eggs were whisked. Bread was buttered and slid into the oven. She made a second pot of coffee.

She oriented the knives in a deliberate but non-threatening way, noting which ones were missing and which remained.

It felt strange to be watched while she cooked, but nearly anything was better than trying to have a conversation that she didn't mean. She let her mind wander to solidify her plan for the night ahead. Logan had made a grave error locking her in the basement with her tools and her prepper supplies. He had underestimated her, and she would use that.

Kate set the table: three sunny yellow plates with corresponding flatware, a pie-shaped third of a fluffy omelet for each of them with cheese and veggies oozing out, a platter of crispy bacon strips, and another of buttered toast. She added a jar of homemade blackberry jam from the fridge to the table and poured a glass of OJ for each of them.

The threesome awkwardly sat at the table to eat.

"How's school going, Ariel?" Logan inquired.

Ariel made a show of slowly chewing, pointing at her mouth to indicate it was full. When she finally swallowed, she replied, "It's good. I did two years in one last year – Mom has been homeschooling me."

"Homeschooling!" Logan said in the same voice someone might use to declare that a turd had indeed been found in the punch bowl. "I don't approve of that. You need to be socialized. You'll go back to public school this year," he decreed.

Ariel clenched her jaw, paused – was she mentally counting to three? – and nodded. "I'd like that."

Kate nodded too, filing it away as one more thing he'd never get to decide for them.

Logan directed his attention to Kate. "Are you still working for that car dealership?"

"Indirectly," she replied. "I process warranty claims for that dealership and a few more. I work from home so I can be there for Ariel."

He nodded his approval. "That's good. A woman should be home for her family."

Kate forced herself to smile as if she was happy to get his approval.

Logan pushed his chair back and patted his stomach. "I'd forgotten what a great cook you are, Katie. That was delicious."

"Thanks," Kate said, smiling limpidly, while longing to have poisoned him.

Ariel got up to return to her room. Logan stopped her. "Where are you going?" he demanded.

Ariel paused, then fell into her role with dramatic fervor. "I'm reading the best book," she told him breathlessly. "I have to get back to it – everyone is about to be killed in an avalanche."

Logan chuckled, buying it hook, line, and sinker. "You were always such a bookworm. I missed you, sweetie."

"Yeah," said Ariel, before she raced from the room. Deceit was difficult for her, and that was usually a good thing. But not today.

Kate poured two more cups of coffee and said, "Let's drink this out on the screen porch."

Logan sat in one of the rocking chairs and sighed, lighting up a cigarette. Freedom felt good, and being here with his family felt even better.

"You always loved it here," Kate said, making small talk, glancing at his hands gripping the mug. They were scarred now, hard and calloused. His arm, beneath the rolled-up sleeve of his flannel shirt, was covered with poorly done tattoos, ink he had not had before going to prison.

"Yep," Logan agreed, yawning. He was tired, Kate observed. She could use that against him later. "I thought of nothing else but being here again with you and Ariel while I was inside. Maybe we could move out here full-time."

She fought the urge to be sarcastic. Old Kate had not been sarcastic. New Kate was just going to have to bite her tongue for a while longer. "Maybe," she submitted. "But it would be hard – I need internet to do my job, and I'd have to commute back to the city once a week to pick up and return paperwork. It might not work out right away, but we could have it as our long-term game plan."

He nodded as he lit a cigarette and put it to his lips.

"When did you start smoking?" Kate asked.

Logan smiled, rocking. Once upon a time, she'd found that smile endearing. Now it just made her want to fling hot coffee on him. She rocked too, forcing herself to concentrate on the morning concerto of the woodland birds instead.

"There's not much to do in prison," he replied. "And smoking there means you can afford smokes, which means you are owed respect.

"I see," she nodded.

They sat in agreeable silence, listening as the forest around them came to life, ignorant of her plight.

It won't be long now, Kate told herself. *He'd better enjoy it here while he can.*

Chapter 12

The day dragged along for Ariel and Kate, but Logan seemed to be having the time of his life. Back was the charming man whom Kate had originally fallen for and whom Ariel had accepted as part of the family. He laughed easily, told familiar stories, and moved through the cabin with proprietary ease—as though the past few years had simply been an unfortunate interruption rather than an exile in prison.

They spent the afternoon playing some board games – Kate had all the classics like Monopoly, Scrabble, and Trouble – while they munched on snacks that Kate had stashed at the cabin.

To anyone peeking through a window who didn't know their background, they looked like an all-American happy family.

Instead, they were part of a hostage situation.

But even in something as simple as an afternoon of board games, little hints of his controlling behavior were evident. Logan insisted on being the banker during Monopoly, sliding the brightly colored paper money across the table with exaggerated fairness. Kate noticed his need to be in charge, even in something so trivial, the way he counted and recounted the bills, corrected Ariel over imagined infractions, and smirked when he won a round in Trouble.

After a lunch of home-canned soup and sandwiches, Logan said, "I need to go get my truck and my supplies. Ariel, let's go for a hike."

Ariel froze, her breath catching, eyes wide as she shook her head and took an unconscious step back, her hands trembling at her sides. Her reaction was instant and visceral—pure animal fear that no amount of acting lessons could hide.

Kate put herself between Logan and her daughter. Her stance was deliberate and unyielding. She wanted to bide her time and enact her plan on the original timeline, but Logan going someplace alone with Ariel was the hill she was ready to die on.

"Absolutely not," Kate told him fiercely. "You want me to trust you, but you want to take my child like you did once before? There's no way, Logan. We'll wait here while you go get your things. You can lock us in the basement again. You can zip tie us. Whatever you need to do, but you are NOT taking Ariel with you."

Logan's face darkened, a flash of rage quickly masked by a forced chuckle. "So that's the story you're telling yourselves about what happened. No wonder Ari's scared to death of me."

Kate glared back at him stubbornly, refusing to give an inch.

"I could just take her, you know," Logan's voice was low and threatening.

It wasn't a bluff. Kate knew. The statement wasn't

meant to persuade—it was meant to remind her of his power.

Kate held his gaze unblinkingly. "Yeah, and ruin any chance of us ever trusting you again."

Logan's eyes narrowed, calculating. After a tense silence, he spoke, his voice calm but edged with steel. "Ari, give me your shoes and get in the basement. Katie, you're with me. I don't trust you two alone—not yet."

Kate turned to Ariel, her heart twisting at the terror in her daughter's eyes. "It's okay, sweetheart," she said softly, forcing calm into her voice. "Do what he says. I'll be fine, I promise."

"You can't promise that," Ariel disagreed, fat tears rolling down her cheeks. "I want to be with you, Mom."

"I'm only taking one of you with me," stated Logan firmly. "You two can thrash it out, but I'm not in the mood to have you plotting against me again."

Kate went to Ariel and hugged her, whispering, "This is how we get out tonight. Trust me."

Ariel's body shook with silent sobs, but she lifted her chin, forcing herself to move. She swapped her boots for the Yeti slippers, clutched her book to her chest like a life preserver, and paused at the basement door. Kate was pleased to see a flicker of defiance flash in her eyes before she descended. Defiance trumped defeat any day of the week.

Ariel paused and looked back at her mother longingly. "I love you, Mom." Her voice broke, and she went downstairs.

Logan rolled his eyes at their dramatic farewell and slammed the basement door's heavy bar into place, the sound echoing in the quiet cabin. Kate laced up her hiking boots, her fingers steady despite the knot in her stomach. She grabbed a water bottle from the fridge, slipped it into her backpack, and followed Logan out the door. The forest loomed beyond the cabin, its dense shadows swallowing the fading daylight.

...

Kate's pulse quickened as Logan led her down the gravel driveway, the stones crunching underfoot in the oppressive silence of the woods. At the bottom, where she expected to turn left toward the main road, Logan veered right. The road narrowed to a single, rutted lane, branches scraping the sides as the forest closed in. A short distance later, he led her off into a thicket, revealing his truck. The diesel pickup was barely visible under a tarp strewn with branches, camouflaged so well she'd never have spotted it.

His preparation chilled her. He hadn't stumbled onto this—he'd planned it. Thought it through.

Kate stood aside while Logan cleared off the truck and unlocked it with his key fob.

"Get in," he ordered.

She climbed into the passenger side, and the cold leather of the seat felt like it was leaching the warmth from her body. The truck reeked of cigarette smoke. She found the back of the cab had been crammed with totes, backpacks, and grocery bags, some coiled rope (what the heck was that for?), and a glint of metal peeking from one (and what the heck was *that*?). He was geared up for the long haul, she realized, her throat tightening.

Kate took a steadying breath. "Can I ask you something?"

Logan's jaw tightened, his eyes narrowing with barely concealed annoyance before he forced a thin smile, his control unnervingly precise. "Shoot."

Don't I wish, thought Kate bitterly. "Aren't you on parole or something? Don't you have to check in, stay away from us?"

"They stole three years from me," Logan answered, his voice low and venomous. "I'm done playing their games."

"But if you don't—" Kate began.

"Enough," he snapped, his hand shoving the key into the ignition. "Q&A time is over." The diesel engine roared to life, drowning out any reply Kate may have made.

Kate clamped her mouth shut and stared straight ahead. Her gut twisted with suppressed rage, but she forced herself to stay calm. If she pushed him too far now, he'd never lower his guard tonight. She had to play this right for Ariel's sake, she counseled herself wisely.

Logan backed out onto the road. He drove back to the cabin in complete silence, with no radio or conversation to break the tension.

...

The short drive back to the cabin appeared to have restored Logan's good mood. "Help me bring this stuff in," he demanded as he shouldered a duffel bag and grabbed a case of beer.

Kate looked away when she saw the beer, because the spark of light in her eyes might give her away. She grabbed the carton of cigarettes that was resting on the center console.

Alcohol. Cigarettes. Fatigue. Overconfidence. Check. Check. Check.

The missing piece of her plan had just fallen into place.

...

The heavy bolt of the basement door scraped open, and Ariel rushed up the stairs into Kate's arms. They clung to each other in the dim cabin, as if they'd been apart for years, not less than an hour.

Logan smirked, shaking his head as if amused, while he shoved beer cans into the vintage refrigerator.

He dug in his backpack and pulled out a bottle in a brown paper bag – some kind of booze, Kate noted, though she wasn't sure what.

Kate forced her face into a neutral expression, suppressing an ebullient smile. With all of that alcohol, he was doing half the work for her. She excused herself to the bathroom.

Once Kate had locked the door behind her, she painstakingly opened the mirrored door to the medicine cabinet. She stopped it before it began to squeal in protest, reaching up along the top shelf for a small bottle of pills she had stashed there for emergencies.

"Alprazolam," the bottle read. "Alcohol may intensify the effects of this medication."

Thanks for the serving suggestion, Kate thought, as she stuffed a few pills into the pocket of her sweatpants, her heart racing with the weight of what she was about to do.

These pills had been in the cabinet for quite some time. They'd been prescribed when Ariel was suffering regularly from uncontrollable panic attacks. She rarely used the pills anymore, but Kate kept them on hand, just in case they were needed.

And today, they were definitely needed.

For good measure, she added a couple of Benadryl tablets to her pocket. She carefully, quietly, closed the door to the medicine cabinet, wincing at the faint click. She flushed the toilet then quickly washed her hands, the sink's gurgle too loud in her ears.

She emerged from the bathroom, carefully schooling her face into the picture of innocence.

Phase two was about to begin.

Chapter 13

As the afternoon rolled toward evening, Kate suggested a cookout around the fire pit. This worked perfectly for her plan, as it would give her a little bit of quality time alone in the kitchen with Logan's beer and the bottle she had now identified as rum. The pills she had hidden felt like they were burning holes through her pocket. The festive atmosphere she hoped to create would lull Logan into a feeling of being accepted.

If there was one thing she'd learned, it was that predators relaxed fastest when they believed they'd already won.

While he and Ariel got the bonfire going in the pit, Kate puttered around the kitchen, making one tray with hot dogs and fixings and another with the components for 'smores. She placed both of the trays in the refrigerator. Then she popped outside with a large bowl and rapidly filled it with wild blackberries.

Her hands moved on autopilot, the familiar rhythm of picking fruit oddly at odds with the cold, clinical calculation going on in her head.

Once inside, Kate broke out the blender. She washed the berries and made virgin daiquiris for herself and Ariel. Then she made an "extra special" drink for Logan. She added blackberries, sugar, a generous serving of rum, and lime juice to the blender pitcher.

The scent of crushed berries and sharp lime filled the small kitchen, bright and summery, masking her darker purpose.

Checking out the window to see that Logan was still outside with Ariel, she pulled an alprazolam tablet from her pocket and cut it in half. It wouldn't do for him to feel like he'd been drugged immediately. She needed to be patient. She added half the pill and a Benadryl to the blender, and then whirred it together with some ice from the freezer. She poured Logan's drink into a large dark green cup with a lid and a straw. She took a small sip to see if the meds were noticeable in the drink. She nodded when she discovered they were well-hidden by the alcohol, berries, and sugar.

She took a tray containing Ariel's baby blue travel cup, her own pink one, and Logan's green cup down to the fire and said, "Surprise!" She pasted a big, goofy smile on her face. "I figured you two worked up a thirst down here, so I made daiquiris with our blackberries. I thought we could have a drink before we made hot dogs."

She pitched her voice to sound breezy and playful, the way Old Kate used to sound on vacation weekends.

Logan smiled back, the old smile that had first won her over. It was boyish, a little embarrassed, and humble-looking. Little did she know then what that charming grin hid, but now she was under no such delusions. She smiled back shyly, forcing back a grimace.

They all sat down in an Adirondack chair and watched the flames while sipping their drinks. "This is delicious, Katie," praised Logan as he savored the drink. "I love that it has our blackberries in it."

Inwardly, Kate winced at his use of the word "our" but she covered it with a smile. "I thought it would make it a nice welcome home drink to use the fruit that grows wild here." The words welcome home nearly choked her, but she managed to make them sound soft, nostalgic.

Logan looked emotional. He fixed his eyes on the fire and reached over to take Kate's petite hand into his big, calloused one. She willed herself not to yank her hand away, and the three sat in companionable silence, watching the flames dance as the forest around them grew darker. His hand felt like the weight of an anchor as he held hers, and it was hard for her to focus on anything but that. Her own palm began to sweat.

To escape the unwanted affection, she got up and collected the cups, returning to the kitchen. She grabbed the hotdog tray from the fridge, tucked some campfire forks under her arm, and carefully took the items down to the fire. She had Ariel grab the forks from under her arm and handed the tray to Logan. "Be right back!" she chirped in a cheery voice. Ariel stared at the long-tined hot dog fork a little too adoringly, and Kate gave her a discreet nudge with her elbow, flashing a warning glance at the girl.

Ariel rolled her eyes and proceeded to space hot dogs out on the forks so that she and Logan could roast them. Satisfied, Kate returned to the kitchen for round two of daiquiris.

She washed out the blender pitcher before making drinks for herself and Ariel, then added the other half of the sedative to Logan's drink, spiking it heavily with rum. She returned to the fire and handed out drinks. Logan looked very, very relaxed. She hid a little smile. *Just wait*, she thought, *this is a night you'll never forget.*

The slight lag in his responses, the looseness in his posture—all of it fed her cautious hope.

Once the hot dogs were ready – Kate's burned until they were black and crispy on the outside, Logan's lightly browned and bubbling, and Ariel's somewhere in between the two– everyone dressed their own buns with mustard, ketchup, and some of the dill pickle relish Kate had canned last summer.

Kate and Ariel broke their hot dogs in half to let the heat escape, but Logan dove right in, sucking in a pained breath as he burned his tongue. That didn't stop him, though, and he inhaled the rest of the hot dog in short order. He was already cooking his third and fourth hot dogs by the time Kate and Ariel finished their first ones.

"Save room for 'smores!" Kate cautioned merrily. Then she began to talk, to share with Logan what he'd missed while he was in jail. She told him how Ariel had won both the English award and the Creative Writing award. She let him know that Ariel had been honored by being chosen to read her patriotic essay about the USA at a Veterans Day event. Ariel had flown by herself to Arizona, where her adoring grandparents picked her up from the Phoenix Airport and spoiled her rotten for three weeks while Kate put in extra hours at work to cover the vacations of others.

Logan's eyes narrowed as he sipped his drink, his words slurring faintly. "I don't like her traveling alone, Kate. Anything could've happened." His gaze flicked to Ariel, heavy with control. "That won't happen again. Not while I'm here. I'll make sure she's safe."

Kate's stomach twisted, but she forced a smile, pressing her foot gently on Ariel's to keep her quiet.

"That's really nice of you, Logan," Kate said. "It's so obvious that you love my daughter. Right, Ariel?"

Ariel gave a pained nod, and Kate prayed that Logan didn't notice her lack of enthusiasm. She quickly changed the subject to something less controversial before she returned to the kitchen to grab the s'mores tray and rejoin them at the fire pit.

Ariel speared marshmallows with practiced ease, then added her "secret" peanut butter to the graham crackers.

Kate offered another round of drinks. Logan hesitated, slurring, "I should switch to beer. I haven't had alcohol in years – three to be exact – and this is hitting hard."

"One more?" Kate coaxed, her voice sweet but her

pulse racing. "It's a celebration."

Ariel didn't realize that Logan was being drugged, but she knew a plot was afoot and she was nothing if not a team player. She chimed in, "Please, Logan? One more with me? Pretty please with blackberries on top?"

Logan chuckled, relenting. He loved being the center of attention and seeing how much his girls seemed to adore him. "Okay, one more and that's it. Otherwise, I'm going to think you're trying to get me drunk and take advantage of me, Katie." He said the last with a comic waggling of his dark brows.

She repressed a shudder and collected the cups. "Be right back!" she chirped cheerfully as she headed back up to the cabin.

In the kitchen, Kate blended his final drink, slipping in a full alprazolam tablet and a Benadryl, masking them with extra rum and sugar. A quick taste confirmed the drugs were undetectable. Her hands shook just enough that she had to pause and breathe before she snapped the lid onto the blender. There would be no undo button after this.

She carried the drinks back down to the fire pit and chatted flirtatiously while watching Logan's eyelids get heavier and heavier. After they enjoyed the gooey s'mores and their final drinks, she yawned outrageously and said, "Wow, I think I'm ready for bed. I assume you're putting us back in the basement tonight?"

"You can stay upstairs with me, Katie," Logan slurred with a sideways grin.

"No, I'm not ready for that yet," Kate stared directly into his eyes. "I need you to be patient with me. If we're really starting over, I need you to respect me. I'd like to stay with Ariel."

Logan opened his mouth to debate, but paused, looking confused. He was too buzzed to form much of an argument, so he yawned instead. The sedatives were beginning to drag him down, smoothing the sharp edges off his temper and his focus.

Kate added a scoop of sand from the bucket beside the fire pit to smother the flames. Once they were out, she took a small shovel she had for just this purpose to spread out the glowing embers and topped them with more sand. She took about five minutes to ensure the fire was completely out, put the lid on, and then the trio made their way back up the short hill to the cabin. She managed to whisper some instructions to Ariel while Logan was concentrating on not stumbling.

Finally, Kate took a deep breath and hooked her arm in Logan's to help him remain upright the last 20 feet to the cabin.

Once they returned, Ariel used the bathroom first, brushed her teeth, and donned her sleeping attire. Tonight she wore a big navy blue t-shirt with a slogan from The X-Files emblazoned across the front. "The Truth Is Out There," the shirt proclaimed over a grainy photo of a UFO. Thick socks were on her feet, black sweatpants covered her legs, and she wore her Yeti slippers again.

Kate quickly washed her face and brushed her teeth. She wore a pair of black sweatpants with a couple of bleach spots on the right leg, topped by a T-shirt that proclaimed "Black Is the New Black" in black letters on black fabric. Socks and slippers also adorned her feet.

She and Ariel didn't argue when Logan escorted them to the basement door. He kissed them both on the cheek, and they hugged him back, hiding their distaste. If they stiffened up a little under his affectionate embrace, he was too disoriented from the drugs and alcohol to notice.

Once they were in the basement, they heard the Molly bar drop into place and heavy footsteps above them.

Kate leaned against the wall, closed her eyes, and took a deep, relieved breath. Her pulse still raced, but underneath the adrenaline was something new: a thin, hard line of hope.

Phase 1 had gone exactly as planned, and now, it was time for Phase 2 of the escape plan.

Chapter 14

"Mom, you have to tell me the plan," insisted Ariel in a whisper. "I need to know!"

Kate gave her daughter a one-armed squeeze around her narrow shoulders, the pressure firm and familiar, meant to steady them both. Ariel felt slender beneath her arm, all bone and tension, but solid nonetheless. "I know," Kate said quietly. "Here's what we're going to do."

She quickly outlined her plan, leaving out the riskiest parts, making decisions on the fly about what Ariel needed to know and what she didn't. Some details were better carried alone. Ariel nodded throughout the explanation, her eyes never leaving Kate's face, lips pressed together as she absorbed each piece and tested it against her own instincts. "But what about shoes? We're going to run away in our slippers?"

"Just at first," Kate assured her. "Trust me, I have it covered."

Ariel looked concerned but determined, that familiar mix of youth and grit tightening her jaw. "I trust you, Mom. We've got this."

"We do," agreed Kate. Saying it out loud had helped solidify the plan in her own mind. "Now, try to take a little nap. We need to let Logan get deeper into sleep. If he catches us trying to escape, it'll be much harder to get away later."

Ariel obediently turned over on her side and pulled out the book she was reading. A couple of pages turned, and soon the book slid from its upright position. Ariel's even breathing confirmed that she was asleep, long, measured breaths that Kate counted automatically, the way she had when Ariel was a baby.

Kate herself had no intention of sleeping. Instead, she wanted to think about the past to steel herself for the mission ahead, to remind herself exactly why hesitation was not an option, and to reinforce in her mind who Logan truly was.

...

> She was on her knees on the school steps, sobbing helplessly, her heart pounding so hard she thought it might burst from her chest. The concrete was biting cold through her sweats, seeping into her skin as if the ground itself was punishing her for having trusted the wrong man.
>
> Janice, from the office, looked panicked and was soon joined by the principal and another teacher. They helped Kate to her feet and led her into the office, past Janice's desk and into the private room that served as the principal's personal office, their voices distant, their hands careful, like she might shatter if touched too firmly.
>
> "Do we need to call the police? Is this a kidnapping?" The principal was Mr. Shelley, a tall, thin man with sad blue eyes, a kindly face, and a pos-

ture that hinted at a military background. He questioned her gently, as if softness alone could undo what had already happened. "Go get her a bottle of water," he told someone behind Kate in a soft voice.

The rest of it was a blur. Kate sipped the water and tried to get a grip on herself. She had already been a mess when she got there, with burst blood vessels in her eyes from the attack, her unbrushed hair wild. Vivid bruises had begun to appear on her arms from where Logan had held her down, finger-shaped shadows blooming beneath her skin. Now, her face was puffy, wet, and red from crying, her feet were still bare, and she was certain she looked like a lunatic who'd just escaped an asylum.

When a female police officer arrived, Mr. Shelley left the room and quietly closed the door behind him. "I'm Detective Harris," she introduced herself. "You can call me Joan. I'm here to help you find your daughter."

Instead of sitting behind the desk, Joan had sat in the chair right beside Kate. She put her hand on Kate's arm, warm, solid, and intentionally human. "It looks like you've had a run-in with someone, too. Can you tell me what happened?"

Kate shook her head frantically. "I don't care about me! He has my daughter!" The words tore from her throat, all pretense at composure gone.

"I understand," Joan had said patiently, kindly. "But I need the whole story to find her."

So Kate told her everything, including the details about the attack. She was too worried about Ariel to feel embarrassed. A few times during the retelling, Joan made a quick call on her cell to provide information to the officers searching for Ariel and Logan. Kate nearly jumped out of her skin when every phone in the office suddenly blared in unison.

It was an Amber Alert.

For her own, beloved Ariel.

In the future, Kate would never hear that sound without thinking of this terrible time and feeling kinship with the mother or father who was desperately searching for their own child, their entire world suddenly reduced to one singular, unbearable fear.

Kate found herself rather unwillingly carted off to the hospital for a forensic exam. Joan had insisted. "When we find him, we want all the evidence we can get to put him away for as long as possible."

Stoically, Kate endured the humiliating exam, thinking only of Ariel. She refused to retreat into shame or shock. She couldn't remember the nurse's name who'd performed the intimate examination, collecting evidence from her body, but she did remember that the woman had a gentle voice, dark skin, and a round, cherubic face. She had been very, very kind.

After the exam, Kate was given a couple of shots and a little cup full of medication. She flatly refused sedation, wanting to be alert in case she could help in the search for her daughter. What if sleep stole precious hours she could be aiding in the search, or silenced a critical phone call that sought vital information only she could supply? The nurse gently washed her face and tended to her bruises and abrasions. They wanted to admit her overnight for observation, but she couldn't possibly lie in a hospital bed while Ariel was out there with the animal she had brought into their lives.

She left against medical advice, called an Uber, and went straight to the police station.

There, she waited outside Joan's office, stubbornly refusing a ride home. She intended to wait until they had Ariel back. She wanted to be in the center of the action, close enough to feel useful. She learned from Joan that Logan had previously had restraining orders from other women, that his behavior now was part of a trend.

She felt sick, thinking of her own poor judgment, of the quiet red flags she'd ignored, of how she had invited a monster into their home. She rushed to the bathroom, but since she hadn't eaten in nearly a day, only dry heaves wracked her body.

Finally, in the wee hours after midnight, Joan came to sit beside her in one of the uncomfortable lobby chairs. "Kate, you need to go home and get some rest. Let me drive you, because I have to go home and get some rest, too. I need to be fresh to follow new leads tomorrow, but I swear to you, I will call you the second I know anything, no matter how small. Let's go."

At the apartment building, Joan walked upstairs with Kate. Investigators had been there and collected evidence. Her home was turned upside down. Her bedding was gone. A film of fine black powder covered the hard surfaces in her bedroom. Everywhere she looked, signs of violation lingered. Kate took some clean clothes from a drawer and shut the door to her room, slamming it. "Do you need a hotel?" Joan asked gently.

"No, I just need a shower. I'm going to lie down in Ariel's room." She saw the doubt on Joan's face and gave her a wry smile. "I'm okay. Really. Get some rest."

Once she had locked the door behind Joan, she got in the shower and turned the water as hot as she could stand. She took a loofah and scrubbed her *skin until it hurt. She put on the soft, thick sweatpants and shirt she'd grabbed from her room and combed out her hair.*

She went into Ariel's room and sat down on the edge of the bed. She took in the photographs, the frenetically colorful posters and artwork, and the huge stacks of books. She tucked herself into Ariel's bed, which smelled like the soap her daughter liked, fresh and herby. There, the tears began to fall, at first gently, then wild and deep, wracking her entire body painfully.

Finally, she slept.

...

Kate shook herself out of her reverie about the longest three days of her life, the memory settling into her bones like jet fuel.

"Never again," she said aloud in a fierce whisper. "Never again."

Maternal rage stoked to full strength, it was time to put her plan into action. She got up and went over to her toolbox to start working on getting out of this basement.

She grabbed a hammer and a roll of dull silver tape, allowing herself a small smile at the prepper's ubiquitous duct tape. Then she turned to her supplies to look for some makeshift weapons. If somehow Logan roused from his drugged state, she would be prepared to fight all the way to the death.

Moonlight shone invitingly through the small, high basement window, and Ariel slumbered on, peacefully unaware of what had been stoked to life in her mother.

Chapter 15

First things first.

Kate grabbed a couple of Ariel's old backpacks, which she had thankfully stashed away instead of tossing, a decision made years ago out of thrift and vague instinct that now felt like providence. A My Little Pony backpack and a purple pack with frolicking kittens would hold their getaway gear, absurdly cheerful choices given the circumstances under which they would be used. What Kate packed wouldn't have to get them far, because she had a secret. She hadn't shared it with Ariel yet, not because she didn't trust her, but because some contingencies worked better if they were invisible.

Into the packs went Lifestraws, empty water bottles, and a couple of sealed pouches of dried fruit. She switched small flashlights on to check the batteries, and those followed. Wool socks, folded trekking poles in little pouches, personal first-aid kits, lighters, and extra bandages rounded out the gear. Two black Arcturus ponchos were pulled out to be worn over the packs—they didn't want to be out in the dark, dark woods with prancing ponies and kittens serving as adorable but dangerous beacons. She loosened the straps of the backpacks until they were all the way extended to fit bigger frames, adjusting them now so there would be no fumbling later.

She stared for a long while at her supplies, wishing fervently for her Glock and the familiar weight and comfort of cold steel. She yearned for an axe, but that was upstairs in the closet on the screen porch, tantalizingly close but utterly unreachable.

Wishes weren't horses, and beggars weren't riding. She would have to make the best of what she had, because waiting for the perfect gear never saved anyone.

A machete, a large knife that could be strapped to her waist over her pajamas, and a larger hammer could serve to defend them. They weren't guns, of course, but she was fueled by mama bear rage, and she was utterly confident in her ability to wield those makeshift weapons with ferocity if it came to that.

She stuffed her feet into her pink, fuzzy slippers, thankful she'd chosen ones with a slightly hard sole that she could wear out on the screen porch on chilly mornings, never imagining this particular use. "Some warrior," she thought with a slightly hysterical giggle.

She gently shook Ariel's shoulder and put her fingers to her lips in a "shhh" sign. Ariel sat up, instantly alert, and nodded. "Wakey wakey, eggs and bakey."

"Wakey, wakey, out we breaky," Ariel replied with an impish grin, humor flaring like a tiny shield. Kate hugged her fiercely. This was her reason why, the reason behind everything she did. She would not fail her daughter.

She instructed Ariel to don the backpack adorned with colorful, dancing ponies. The girl stuck her book into the bag and put it on. She covered up with a poncho, stuffed her feet into her Yeti slippers, and tightened up her ponytail. Ariel wore the same look of resolve that Kate imagined she had on her own face, quiet and determined rather than scared.

Now it was time for the next step of her plan. She used the knife from her hip to cut strips of duct tape, which she applied directly to the glass of the only window in the basement, layer by careful layer, to control the breakage and muffle it. She quietly moved a stepladder to the high window and tossed a blanket from their bed on the floor below it. She took another blanket, liberated from her supplies, applied rolled-up duct tape to that, and then secured it to the glass.

She took a step back and looked at the tape and padding she had installed. She could think of no other way to make breaking a window quieter.

It was time. She trusted her preparations.

Taking her hammer, she struck the padded glass. There was a small thunk, but certainly nothing that would wake up Logan. However, she was going to have to hit it a lot harder than that to break the window. She donned heavy work gloves and swung the hammer with all her might. It still didn't shatter, but she heard a soft crack. She swung again and was rewarded by the loosening of the blanket and tape as the window quietly gave way. The duct tape prevented it from crashing to the floor. Another swing in the other corner, and Kate was certain the glass was thoroughly destroyed.

She stepped to the side and carefully pulled away the blanket. The duct tape sagged but held all the shards of glass. She wiggled it to pull the glass from the frame and smiled when the pine-scented breeze entered the basement room.

Success.

Carefully, she folded the duct tape shield over so the broken glass was in the middle and set it aside.

She used her heavy gloves to pull the last few shards of glass out of the window frame. She didn't want either of them getting hurt or leaving a trail of blood that could be easily followed, especially not now.

The blanket she'd put on the floor to catch any glass that fell hadn't been needed for that purpose, so she used it to pad the bottom frame of the window, softening it into something easier to pass through.

"Be careful," she warned Ariel in a whisper. "There's still a little bit of glass I couldn't get out of the frame."

Ariel nodded, determination writ large on her face. She climbed up the stepladder and wriggled through the window, backpack and all. There was a grating sound as she made her way through, and her poncho briefly caught on the rough top of the window frame. But then she was out, breathing free air, eyes shining in the moonlight.

Kate knew she would absolutely not fit through that window with all her gear, so she handed the poncho, backpack, machete, and two hammers out to her daughter.

It was a much tighter squeeze as she labored her way through the gritty sill. She had a moment of horror when it looked like she wasn't going to make it through, but finally she toppled out into the grass with her daughter. She lay there for a moment, lungs burning, torso abraded, but victorious.

Quietly, she donned the kitten backpack and covered it with the poncho. She desperately wanted to peek through the living room window to make sure Logan was still sleeping and not lying in wait for them in the dark forest. She knew she was more likely to get caught that way, in the event he was getting up to go to the bathroom or just happened to rouse from his sleep and glance out the window. She squelched that nearly irresistible urge, handed one hammer to Ariel, then picked up the other hammer and the machete. Thus armed, she headed toward freedom with her daughter.

"Where are we going?" whispered Ariel so quietly that she could barely be heard. "It isn't safe to try and go down this mountain to Mr. Slocum's in the dark."

"That's why we're not going down the mountain," Kate replied softly. "We're going up."

She turned Ariel's shoulders to face a steep path behind the cabin. "This way. This hill is our haven, and it will protect us. Trust me."

"Off we go, me and my Yeti slippers, straight up Haven Hill!" Ariel smiled bravely in the darkness.

"Off we go, little warrior," Kate smiled back.

Quietly, the two made their way to the path and disappeared into the trees, with only the glowing moon lighting their way, leaving the false safety of the walls behind for the honest danger of the wild.

Chapter 16

Kate and Ariel walked without a word for at least ten minutes. The moonlight, which might have given them away earlier in their escape, now allowed them to move through the forest without turning on flashlights.

The slippers they wore protected their feet to some degree, but they were careful to avoid the sharp rocks they saw, placing each step with deliberate caution. The path was steep, and they needed all their concentration to navigate it in fuzzy house shoes that had no grip. It forced them to slow down even when instinct urged them to speed up.

Finally, the path leveled off a little. They sat down, side by side, on a fallen branch, knees bent, shoulders touching, to catch their breath. They spoke quietly, because sound traveled in these mountains at night, and neither of them wanted to test just how far it could carry.

"Why are we going up, Mom?" asked Ariel. "Where are we going?"

"I have a cache just a little further ahead, and it has things we might need. Plus," Kate paused for a moment, then continued, choosing her words with care, "we don't want to do what is expected. Logan may not wake up until morning, but if he realizes we're gone sooner, the first place he's going to look for us is the trail to the Slocum place. Also, searchers—professional or not—always go downhill first."

Ariel nodded, absorbing the logic rather than just the reassurance. "So we're going to hang out on the mountain for a while?"

While they talked, Kate pulled a small bundle from each backpack. As she unfolded the trekking poles, they made a loud SNAP as the pieces joined together. She cringed each time. It sounded like the crack of a gunshot in the quiet, midnight forest. But they'd be needed to safely navigate the next part of the trail in their bedroom slippers. Extra points of contact mattered more than silence right now, and Kate was willing to accept the trade-off, even though it set her nerves on edge.

She handed Ariel a small flashlight and tucked the other light into her own pocket.

"Yes, but just until midday tomorrow. He'll have looked for us early, but I don't think he'd ever imagine we'd go further up into the woods. Are you ready to go a little bit further?"

Ariel hopped up and flexed her muscles. "Let's blow this popsicle stand."

Kate handed her the purple pair of trekking poles. "Let's make like a tree and leave."

"We're going to make like a rock and roll."

"Let's be like a ball and bounce."

"We're out like trout."

With a couple of quiet giggles, quickly stifled, the two returned to the trail. It cut the tension just enough to help them feel a little calmer about their situation.

Soon, the path narrowed until it was hardly noticeable. The hiking became more difficult as it steepened. Even though they were both accomplished hikers, doing this in the dark and without the proper footwear was a lot more treacherous than their usual outings. "Go slowly," Kate cautioned Ariel, who was clambering up ahead of her. "We're not in any rush. We're not being followed."

"Okay, slowpoke," teased Ariel. "I'll let you catch up."

The trekking poles helped a lot, Kate thought, wincing as she felt her foot slip and land on something sharp, pain blazing through her heel. Finally, they reached the point where the ground leveled off again. Kate veered to the right, with Ariel close behind her.

They walked another ten minutes or so, struggling through the thick brush. Ariel walked right past the cave entrance, which Kate took as a good sign. "Psst," she whispered. "Back here."

She pulled aside the ever-present kudzu that hid the mouth of the cave and shone her flashlight into the darkness just to make sure no creature of the forest had taken up residence in her cache. When she confirmed it was vacant, she slipped in, her daughter close behind her. Both of them were careful not to disturb the vines any more than necessary.

Once inside, she took a lighter out of her backpack and lit the tea light candle in the glass lantern stuffed into a ledge near the entrance to the cave. It looked totally empty, even with the light of the lantern. Ariel sat down gratefully, glad for the respite from the arduous hike.

Kate headed straight to the back of the shallow cave. Holding her LED flashlight between her teeth, she moved a gray camouflage tarp that blended with the wall so well it was practically invisible. Ariel watched with great interest as her mother revealed a stack of yellow, 4-gallon Tidy Cats litter buckets. She'd be willing to bet that her mom had not secretly dragged up 35-pound buckets of kitty litter, and she was curious to see what treasures had been hidden away, her fatigue momentarily forgotten.

Kate opened the first bucket and tossed Ariel a full water bottle and a little yellow bag. Ariel gasped in delight when she saw it was a bag of peanut M&Ms. Kate sat down with her own snack and guzzled the water. She wasn't worried about conserving—there were more filled bottles, and she knew of a mountain creek nearby. She pulled another water bottle out of the bin and drank it more slowly.

With a weary sigh, Kate pushed herself up from the floor. "I don't know about you," she said to Ariel, "but I'm beat."

"Same. I—" Ariel interrupted herself with a huge yawn, and they both giggled.

Kate dug into another bucket, frowned, and opened a third bucket. "Yes!" she rejoiced. She pulled out two tightly wrapped sleeping bags and a couple of other mysterious, lumpy bundles. While Ariel was spreading out the sleeping bags, Kate opened the bucket at the back. She pulled out a gun box holding a Glock 19, two boxes of ammunition, and some magazines for the pistol. This should even the playing field, she thought with satisfaction. The familiar equipment restored a sense of balance.

In the final bucket, Kate pulled out two pairs of hiking boots. They were the ones she and Ariel had retired when they got new ones, but they still had life in them, and Ariel's feet hadn't changed sizes in a couple of years. She also retrieved socks and a cozy sweatshirt for each of them.

The lumpy things were vacuum-packed pillows. Ariel fluffed them up while her mother put the lids back on the kitty litter containers. "Where did you get all those buckets?" Ariel asked. "We don't even have a cat."

"A lady two floors up in our building is always putting her empty buckets into the recycling bin. I just grabbed a few," Kate replied, muffling her own yawn. "They're waterproof, crushproof, and they don't smell like food. Oh, and they're free."

Ariel settled into her sleeping bag. She put on her headlamp and pulled her book out of her backpack.

Kate put on her own headlamp and proceeded to load her magazines with ammo. Once she was done, she saw that Ariel had fallen fast asleep mid-page. She gently removed the book from her daughter's hands and folded down the corner of the page she had been on. She gazed at the girl, filling up on how much she loved her, quietly memorizing the moment. Then she switched off Ariel's headlamp and got into her own sleeping bag.

She didn't think she'd get a wink of sleep out there in a cave on the side of the mountain, but exhaustion proved her wrong. She didn't even remember turning off her headlamp.

Chapter 17

When Kate awakened, dappled sun shone on the wall of the cave, and she couldn't remember where she was for a moment. She went to stretch and was momentarily confined by the sleeping bag, which brought her to full, panicked wakefulness immediately, her breath catching before she forced it back under control.

The Glock was right there beside her, like a silent guardian. The sight of it grounded her, anchoring her back in the present. She felt the hard, unforgiving floor of the cave beneath her and winced as she sat up gingerly. She smiled to herself. She knew that Ariel would bounce right up with the resilience of a young person, making her feel even older.

She wriggled out of the bag, stuffed some tissues in her pocket, and strapped the Glock to her waist. She dug her phone out of the backpack, silently swearing at herself for not thinking about looking for service last night.

She went outside to do her business before waking Ariel. She stretched when she got out of the cave, putting her hand on the stony entrance for balance. She was stiff and achy from sleeping on the cold ground. She felt like she'd aged fifty years in one chilly night, every joint protesting the abuse.

Once out of the cave, she squinted up at the sky. The sun was fairly high. They'd slept late. That was okay, though. Exhaustion had caught up with them, whether she liked it or not, and pushing through it now would only invite mistakes.

She figured that the most dangerous time to be out on the trail to Mr. Slocum's house would be in the daylight. Logan would be looking for them as soon as he discovered they'd escaped. And he wouldn't be happy.

Kate's plan was to stay hidden all day if they could, then hike to the neighbor's place just after dusk. Dawn and dusk were always more dangerous times to be out and about in the habitats of wild animals, but here she was, back to that "man or bear" analogy. She'd far rather deal with the wildlife than the crazed stalker that Logan had become. It was far easier to understand the motivation of animals and predict how they would respond. Logan was a volatile wildcard.

She'd shut off the phone to save the battery. Now, she turned it on hopefully. For a second, she saw one bar, and her heart started pounding: service meant rescue. But the connection rapidly disappeared, so fast she wondered if she'd really seen a bar after all. She held the phone up in all directions, desperate for a signal. She turned the device off in disappointment, shoving it into her pocket.

She made her way back into the cave. She liberated a bottled, room-temperature latte, sipping the precious caffeine, glad that she had thought to add these beverages to her cache.

She decided it was best to let Ariel sleep for as much of the day as possible to reduce her stress—or at the very least, the amount of time she was stressed. Kate pulled a crossword puzzle book, a pen, and a deck of cards from one of the kitty litter containers. She rolled the backpack into a makeshift pillow and leaned against the wall, with the bag padding her back. The cave wasn't very big, but she could sit up where the walls curved toward the ground without hunching over, a position that let her watch the entrance without looking obvious.

She was four puzzles deep by the time Ariel began to stir. As predicted, the girl hopped up as though she'd just finished a peaceful slumber on a downy king-sized bed at a five-star hotel. Kate shook her head faintly, equal parts envy and relief.

Ariel followed her mother's example, going outside for a few moments. When she came back, Kate handed her a granola bar and a baggie of dehydrated apple slices. She grabbed the same thing for herself, and the two sat down cross-legged, eating their breakfasts.

"No fire? No coffee?" Ariel raised a curious eyebrow.

"Not hot coffee," replied Kate, shaking a bottled latte in her daughter's general direction. "I'm not going to build a fire or get a scent in the air or do anything else that might draw Logan to us."

"So, what's the plan, Mom?" asked Ariel around a mouthful of chewy granola bar.

"We're going to let him search for us today, then when it begins to get closer to dark, we're going to Mr. Slocum's place, calling the cops, and getting the heck out of here."

"He sure is going to be mad," Ariel mused, a bit of a quaver in her voice. "You really don't think he'll find the cave?"

Kate looked outside the mouth of the cave. She spoke slowly, gravely. "I can't promise that he won't find the cave. But I can promise you that if he does, he will not touch you." She turned back to face her daughter and met her eyes. "I give you my word, I will not let him hurt you. I will not let him take you away again."

Ariel glanced knowingly at the gun that Kate had removed from her holster and put beside her for easier access while she was seated on the floor. Kate saw her gaze and affirmed, "I'll do what I have to do."

Ariel looked away and was silent for a long minute. Then she said, "If you don't, I will. I know what he did to you, too, Mom," she replied. Her voice was strong and unwavering, but her eyes were distant. Her tone was steady, practiced. Too steady. "Can I carry a gun today as well? You know I can shoot the cap off a bottle. You're the one who taught me."

Kate froze. The cave suddenly felt smaller. She hadn't realized that Ariel knew about the brutal sexual assault she had endured at Logan's hands. She had made sure her daughter was not in the courtroom when she had testified about the attack. It took her a moment to gather herself to respond.

"Ari, I don't want you to have to live with something like shooting another human being," Kate stated firmly. "That would be so traumatic for you, and you've already been through so much."

Ariel set her jaw firmly. "It would be better than being helpless if he tried to take me again."

Kate sighed, the sound heavy with more than fatigue. "Let me think about it, okay?" She picked up a deck of cards that sat beside her. "Crazy 8s?"

...

Kate and Ariel spent the afternoon quietly playing cards in the cave. While some might have found it strange that they were playing games while a crazed stalker was in the woods looking for them, it took their mind off their troubles and reduced their stress levels. Stressed people made silly mistakes, so it seemed to Kate it was better to pass the time doing something fun.

When they stepped out to commune with Mother Nature briefly, it felt like a typical summer day, the hot sun beating down between the turning leaves. But inside the cave, it was cool and damp, the air at least twenty degrees cooler than it was outside.

The tension of constantly listening for footsteps drawing near or shouts from down the mountain wore on them, nonetheless. Every snapped branch, every crunch of leaves, had Kate holding her breath, heart racing, hand on the pistol, until she determined it wasn't an immediate threat, then forcing herself to relax again.

She couldn't decide if it was good or bad that she couldn't hear Logan yelling. It was good in that he wasn't too close. It was bad in that she had no idea where he was or what he was doing.

"About that gun, Mom...?" Ariel left the question dangling in the air.

Kate looked at her daughter's earnest face for a moment and came to a decision. She abruptly rose from the floor of the cave. "I'm going to give you pepper spray and a taser, Ariel," she announced. "What you need to know about the taser is that if you're touching him when you tase him, you'll be shocked too. Pepper spray will blow back in your face if the wind is blowing the wrong way. But neither of these will kill anyone or cause long-term harm."

"But, Mom—" Ariel started.

"No gun," Kate interrupted. "That's my final decision."

Ariel looked sulky. "I don't want to play cards anymore." She folded her arms.

"Then read your book," Kate suggested, pretending not to notice her daughter's sullen expression.

"Fine," she huffed, flopping back down on her sleeping bag and picking up her book, her back turned to Kate.

Kate wanted to continue explaining her reasoning to Ariel, but she wisely kept quiet to let the girl sort it out and calm down on her own. Talking would only add fuel to the fire, and Ariel was in no mood to listen to logic, no matter how sound it was.

This would be a good time to repack their bags for the treacherous night hike ahead of them. They needed to move quickly and quietly, and Kate had some special additions she wanted to add to the packs. It would give Ariel some time to cool off while giving Kate something concrete to focus on.

Part of her yearned to stay hidden in the cave until Logan gave up and went away, but she knew, rationally, that this would not be over until she ended it.

And one way or another, she *would* end it.

Chapter 18

While Ariel read, Kate emptied both of their backpacks and sat cross-legged on the floor of the cave by the supplies she had cached away. She spread everything out deliberately, grouping items by use instead of by convenience. When she had created the cache, it hadn't been with Logan in mind. She had been thinking about the "golden horde" she had been warned about in prepper books and forums —waves of desperate urban hipsters looking for food and shelter after fleeing the cities. She'd set this up in case she and Ariel had ever needed to retreat from the cabin.

Whatever the reason she had built it, she was grateful she had set up her little cache. She had made it on a dime, since her budget was tight, and it was serving her well right now, proof that preparations didn't have to be perfect to matter.

The sun was low in the sky, and evening was drawing near. Kate wanted to be ready to go once dusk fell.

She pulled out a couple of cans of ravioli and sporks for a quick meal before they set out. Then she pulled out her weapons stash. An extra gun, a smaller Glock 23, would fit in an ankle holster. She loaded it, then strapped it on above her hiking boot, pulling her sock up to pad her leg. She pulled out the promised taser and pepper spray containers for Ariel, then added one of each to her own arsenal. Three bottles of water, two bags of peanut M&Ms, some sealed packs of dehydrated fruit, rain ponchos, extra socks, and a cozy sweater went into each bag. Lighters, waterproof matches, LED flashlights, and a good multitool filled out the supplies. Personal first aid kits went in, as well as a hat and a pair of gloves for each of them.

Kate tested the weight of the bag—not bad. Heavy enough to be useful, light enough to move with.

She hooked their trekking poles to the outside of each bag to help them navigate the treacherous trail in the dark, then pulled out some bear spray to be clipped to their waists, a large knife for herself and a smaller one for Ariel, and all the magazines she had filled earlier. Was she forgetting something? The thought nagged at her, familiar and unwelcome, but finally she chalked it up to anxiety. She had everything she needed for them to make their escape.

She popped the top of a ravioli can for each of them and set Ariel's can and a spork onto her sleeping bag, where she was still reading with her back turned.

"Yum," she said when she saw the can. "A feast to be coveted!"

"It was made by a short, round chef who sought the finest ingredients and added his own magic to this humble vessel."

Ariel giggled at the seriousness of her mother's face as she described Chef Boy Ar Dee, her good spirits restored by an afternoon of reading.

They ate their pasta cold and then munched on some dried fruit for dessert.

"So, here's the plan," Kate said as their meal came to a close. "We aren't going to take the regular trail to Mr. Slocum's place. If Logan is smart, and unfortunately, he is, he'll be staking it out."

Ariel rolled her eyes at the concept of Logan being smart, but kept silent.

"We're going to go down that trail by the waterfall and come out behind the cabin. There, we can hide for a bit and make sure Logan isn't at Mr. Slocum's. Then we can call the cops, and this will finally be over."

"Sounds good to me," agreed Ariel. "I'm glad you had sweatpants up here—the bugs are going to be after us at that time of night."

"I know. It's not ideal, but it's the best plan I can think of."

Ariel slung her lanky arms around her mother's neck. "It's a great plan, Mom. We've got this."

"Last time, Logan got hold of you behind my back. This time, I want you to walk in front of me, but not too far. We need to stay close to each other," Kate added, choosing her words carefully. Because how on earth do you teach your fourteen-year-old about getting out of the way so you can shoot her captor? she thought.

"If he catches us—catches you—I want you to go limp. Just drop to the ground where he has to hold you up. It will distract him, and it will get you out of my line of fire."

"You're going to shoot him?" Ariel raised a naturally arched brow in question.

"If I have to," Kate replied matter-of-factly.

Ariel nodded, then offered her mother a comforting hand. Kate smiled, then glanced outside. "It's time to go. Are you ready?"

"Ready as spaghetti."

"Ready as a three-legged dog at a fire hydrant."

"Ready as a one-legged man at a butt-kicking contest."

"Ready as a one-eyed cat at a fish pond."

"Ready as... darn it, you won again."

They both giggled, tied up their boots, and grabbed their bags. It was time for the final leg of their escape.

It was strange, walking the trails as the sun was setting. Generally, Kate avoided being in the woods at dusk and dawn because those were the times of day when the local wildlife were most likely to be hunting for prey. Today, it was a choice between the devil and the deep blue sea, and she was choosing the sea.

They hiked along the steep trail, using trekking poles to navigate the more perilous sections. This trail wasn't regularly used and was so faint it would be easy to miss in daylight, much less in the dark. But they had the home-field advantage, and Kate was confident they would not get lost.

As the cloak of night fell heavier on the forest, Kate could occasionally see gleaming eyes in the brush near them. She didn't want to spook Ariel, so she kept it to herself. Just a fox or a raccoon, she told herself. Usually, she liked the feeling of not being alone on the mountain. Still, right now, she fervently wished that the local critters would go on a nice vacation somewhere else. Maybe somewhere tropical, she mused, then choked back a crazed giggle at the thought of bears and foxes on the beach in the Florida Keys.

They had been hiking silently for at least an hour when they heard it.

Logan was shouting for them in the distance, his voice broken and raw, like he'd been yelling their names all day. They both froze, and Ariel turned to face her mother, naked fear in her eyes.

Kate put her mouth right next to Ariel's ear. "Sound travels in these woods. He may not actually be that close. We have to keep going, but do not make a peep."

Ariel nodded that she understood, then stiffened her shoulders and proceeded down the path. They walked as silently as possible, hoping to avoid a confrontation with Logan.

They both naturally slipped into the method for moving through the forest undetected in a course they had taken with a Native American instructor. They were instructed to keep their ankles slightly flexed to land softly. They were to seek out each step ahead with their toes to determine if there was a stick to crack under their weight or a rock that would slide noisily underfoot. Then the step could be taken, paying attention to each part of their foot when it touched the ground.

It was like mother-daughter telepathy as they both began to move stealthily, as they had been taught. It was much harder work to progress silently, and it was far slower than simply striding along. However, it was worth the extra effort to remain undetected. As it grew darker in the forest, they used their trekking poles more to feel out the way ahead of them than for balance. Finally, Logan's voice faded, and Kate signaled Ariel to stop with a hand on her shoulder.

Gratefully, they both sat down right in the middle of the path. A water bottle and a pack of peanut M&Ms hit the spot while they took a break. Kate's legs were throbbing from the effort, and Ariel's must be too. Kate watched her daughter aimlessly rubbing her thighs while snacking.

Kate whispered, "Either he's not yelling anymore, or we're too far away to hear him."

Ariel replied, "It was getting quieter as we walked. I think we're too far away. I bet he'll yell forever; he'll be so mad."

Kate nodded. "It's hard to tell in the dark, but I think we should be coming up to the back of Mr. Slocum's place in the next hour or so," she told her daughter.

Ariel's nod was barely perceptible in the dark. "It feels so strange to be out here without a flashlight."

"It does," her mother agreed.

"But I kind of like it," Ariel continued. "It's like we're reclaiming our mountain from that jerk."

Kate smiled. "I love you, Ari, and I'm so proud of how strong you are."

"Aw, shucks," Ariel whispered back, feigning a strong accent and looking down in a pretend-humble pose.

They both laughed softly, finished their snacks. Kate shoved the empty wrappers in her pocket, and they got up to continue their trek.

They pressed on, the forest around them a maze of shadows and soft creaks. The trail, barely visible in the dark, wound through thickets of rhododendron and pine. In this part of the forest, the air smelled strongly of damp earth and decaying leaves. It was a good smell: earthy, warm, and familiar.

Kate's trekking pole probed the ground ahead, her movements slow and deliberate. Ariel followed suit, stepping lightly over the trail littered with branches, fallen leaves, and pine cones. Kate's heart still raced from Logan's distant shouts, but the silence now was almost worse. It was like the mountain itself was holding its breath, waiting for something to happen.

They were closing in on Mr. Slocum's property, though the dark made every step feel like a roll of the dice. Kate's legs ached, but she pushed the pain aside, focusing on Ariel's silhouette ahead of her. Her daughter's resilience was incredible.

A sudden rustle broke the quiet, heavy and close, from the brush to their right.

Kate froze. She held her breath.

Her left hand shot out to grip Ariel's arm.

Her right hand was aiming the gun she hadn't even remembered drawing.

Ariel stiffened, her breath hitching.

Something—or someone—was there.

Chapter 19

The sound came again, and it was definitely a footstep on the littered terrain of the forest floor. Then she heard a low, huffing snort, followed by the unmistakable crack of a branch under weight.

It was something big.

Kate's pulse spiked as her eyes caught movement—a hulking shape shifting through the trees, its dark fur blending with the night. A black bear, its broad head swinging as it sniffed the air.

Oh boy, thought Kate hysterically. We really are choosing between man and bear.

Ariel's fingers dug into Kate's sleeve, her eyes wide with terror. Kate leaned in, her whisper barely a breath. "Don't run. Stay close."

Ariel nodded, her trembling hand clutching her trekking pole like a weapon.

Kate's mind raced. Black bears in these mountains weren't usually aggressive, but they were drawn to food.

The peanut M&Ms.

The crumbs on their hands, the wrappers in her pocket.

All the little things she should have been more careful about.

Damn it, she thought, cursing her carelessness. The bear's snout lifted, its eyes glinting as it shuffled closer, maybe fifteen feet away, its bulk rustling the undergrowth.

"Raise your poles," Kate whispered, her voice steady despite the fear clawing her chest. She holstered her weapon and switched to her trekking poles. A 9mm wouldn't do much to fend off a bear unless the shot was absolutely perfect. And a wounded bear was a ticked-off bear. "Make yourself big. Move slow."

They lifted their trekking poles high, arms spread to widen their silhouettes. Kate stepped in front of Ariel, using her body as a shield, though her legs felt like jelly, and she had to consciously force herself not to give in to the shaking.

The bear paused, its ears twitching, its heavy breathing audible in the still night. It took a step forward, its claws scraping against a rock, the sound sharp in the silence.

Kate's thoughts whirled like a tornado. Black bears would usually back off if you made a loud noise, but startling them could make things worse. And then there were Logan's irate shouts. If they made a racket, their shouts might lead Logan right to them.

There was no perfect solution.

Ideally, they'd scare it off without giving away their position. But was it worth the risk?

"Get out your bear spray. Back up very slowly," Kate murmured, guiding Ariel with a gentle push.

"Keep facing it. Don't turn your back on it."

They edged backward, Kate's poles still raised, Ariel clutching the can of bear spray like it was a lifeline. The forest floor crunched faintly under their careful steps. The bear snorted again, its dark eyes tracking their movement.

Kate's heart pounded so loudly she was surprised that the entire forest didn't hear it. She could smell the bear's musky scent now, carried on the breeze. This was entirely closer to a bear than she'd ever wanted to be.

The M&M wrapper crinkled in her pocket like a taunt, reminding her that she'd failed to bury her trash.

The bear seemed undeterred by their poles. They had to act and deal with the most imminent threat first.

"We have to scare it," Kate hissed. "There's no choice. Yell, Ari. As loud as you can."

Ariel's voice shook, but came out strong. "Hey! Get out of here! Bad bear!" Kate joined in, her shout fierce despite the fear choking her. "Go on, bear! Get!" They stomped the ground, banging their poles together, their voices echoing off the trees.

The bear froze, its ears flattening. For a heart-stopping moment, it stood its ground, staring at them intently.

From a distance, Logan's voice cracked through the night again, raw and furious, calling their names. The bear's head jerked toward the sound, its body tensing. Kate's stomach dropped. Logan was closer than she'd thought, and his shouting was like a match in a powder keg. The bear huffed, taking another step toward them, its eyes flicking between Kate and Ariel and the direction of Logan.

They had chosen their course and committed to it, continuing their onslaught of noise. They would deal with Logan if they survived the bear encounter.

Finally, the beast let out a low woof and lumbered off, crashing through the brush. Its heavy steps faded into the forest, leaving only the crunch of leaves in its wake. Kate kept yelling until she was sure it was gone, her throat raw. She pulled Ariel into a quick, fierce hug, both of them shaking.

"Is it gone?" Ariel whispered, her voice small against Kate's shoulder.

"Yeah, I think so," Kate said, scanning the darkness. "But Logan's out there, and he probably got a good idea of where we are now. We've got to move."

"I hope the bear will eat Logan," offered Ariel optimistically, in a less tremulous voice.

It broke the tension enough for Kate to laugh. "Me too. That would solve a lot of our problems."

They hurried forward, their stealth sacrificed for speed. The bear was gone, but Logan was not. His shouts were louder now, his rage cutting through the night.

Now he knew for sure that they were out there.

Their beloved mountain had turned into a gauntlet, and they were far from the end of it. Everything felt too close to comfort, like the very trees were closing in on them. The forest they loved so much was different in the shadowy dusk. It was less inviting, more frightening. The hoot of an owl, the crack of a fallen branch—every sound made them jump. Kate tried to make light of the anxiety by laughing softly at their reactions.

But the truth was, they were both scared half to death.

Kate's steps slowed. She had almost forgotten one of the most important survival lessons she'd ever learned:

Don't run FROM danger. Run TO safety.

Despite their panic at Logan's nearness, they had to be smart. They couldn't just run aimlessly around the forest forever.

Kate raced through her options.

Logan would expect them to go to Mr. Slocum's for help. He would cut them off on the trail.

The cave was too far back and all uphill, which would slow them down and wear them out.

There was nowhere to go that seemed like the best option.

But they could hide, bide their time in the forest as close to the Slocum place as possible, and let him run out of energy looking for them.

"We can't go right to Mr. Slocum's," Kate announced softly, stopping dead. Ariel bumped into her, her pole scraping a rock. The noise made Kate's stomach twist, and she scanned the dark, half-expecting Logan to pop out.

Ariel's voice was a shaky hiss. "What? Why not? It's right there, Mom! We're almost there!"

Kate leaned in, voice low. "Logan knows we'd head there. He'll be waiting. We're going to hide and wait him out. He can't stay there staking out the neighbor forever." Even as she said it, she wasn't sure she believed it.

Ariel's eyes went wide, and her jaw tightened, but she gave a quick nod. "Okay. Where do we go?" Ariel asked, barely audible, squaring her shoulders.

Kate looked around, her brain foggy from her recent panic. The trail curved around a steep slope, with thick bushes on one side and large rocks on the other. In the dim moonlight, she spotted a low overhang under a boulder. It was covered by ferns, the ever-present kudzu vines, and some gnarly roots. It was an indent, not an actual cave, and looked just big enough for them to squeeze into.

But it would do the trick and hide them from the trail. They'd only be a quick hike to their neighbor's place, and hopefully, Logan, like the bear, would give up and go away.

"There," Kate said in a low, steady voice, pointing. "We'll sit tight, keep quiet, hide for a while, and rest. I don't know about you, but I'm beat."

They crept up the incline, poles poking for sticks that would give them away. Kate waited while Ariel crawled in first, then she followed, the dirt cold under her hands. Was there a better option? she wondered. It didn't matter, she resolved. They were committing to this plan for now.

Ariel slid in deeper, her elbow knocking a fern loose. Kate shot her a look, fixing it quickly. They tucked their poles close and crammed together in the tight space, the local flora hiding them like the world's flimsiest curtain.

The forest seemed noisy now that they were still—a chorus of crickets, rustling leaves, a creek in the distance. Kate listened hard for Logan—his steps, his voice, anything that would give her an early warning.

She drew her pistol, ready to blow him into the afterlife if she had to. *I've changed,* she thought, *to consider shooting my ex a practical solution instead of a shocking one.*

Ariel shivered, her shoulder pressed against Kate's left side. "How long do we wait?" she whispered, her breath warm in the cool air.

"Till we're sure he's moved on," Kate murmured. "If he's at Mr. Slocum's, he'll get mad and start searching the trails. He's not patient, and we can use it to our advantage. We just need to outlast him. We can do this, honey."

Ariel curled up tighter, nodding. Kate kissed her on top of the head. It was too cold for August, the kind chill that got into your bones and made your teeth chatter. Or maybe that was just the adrenaline. Their legs ached, and Ariel looked utterly exhausted in the darkness. They shared a water, and when she moved, Kate heard that stupid M&M wrapper crinkling in her pocket. She wanted to kick herself for keeping it after the bear fiasco.

The time dragged on, making Kate feel like she was trapped in a slow-motion sequence in a movie. She dozed on and off. Ariel snored softly next to her.

Then, a crunch sounded somewhere down the trail. Kate grabbed Ariel's arm. Quiet, she mouthed. Ariel nodded. She understood.

Another crunch, and this one was closer. Was it Logan? A deer? Another freaking bear? Ariel's fingers tightened on her taser. Kate's pulse hammered, her hands clutching her pistol.

Then she smelled it, an odor that absolutely did not belong. It was the acrid scent of a cigarette wafting through the freshness of the forest.

Chapter 20

Kate froze at the smell of the cigarette wafting through the forest. She knew it had to be Logan, and he must not be very far away if they could smell the smoke from his cigarette out here in the open air.

A mutter reached her ears. It was definitely Logan's voice, too muffled to understand but way too close. When he began talking to himself, she recalled, it was always bad news.

She didn't know whether to be relieved that it wasn't another bear or to wish that it had been her ursine buddy. Logan was searching, probably trying to guess their path, trying to crawl inside her head the way he always had.

The muttering faded, then came back nearer. If he found them, they were stuck. There was no room to bolt. She eyed the slope below, steep and dark, but maybe their only shot for escape if it came to it.

Kate held her breath, certain that the sound of her exhale would draw him nearer. She gripped her pistol in both hands, fully prepared to open fire if he found them. Ariel had pulled out her taser and clung to it like her life depended on it.

Ariel's eyes were wide as they locked on Kate's.

Kate mouthed, *Stay still.*

The crunching stopped. The hair on the back of Kate's neck rose.

Ariel's hand found Kate's arm in the dark.

Kate gave her hand a comforting squeeze, then gently removed it from the embrace. She clutched her pistol with both hands again, aiming outward, fully prepared to end this entire situation if he found their hiding place. She couldn't risk anything that might affect her shot.

They sat frozen as Logan's footsteps crunched again, agonizingly close, then paused. Kate's muscles felt like they were about to stage a rebellion as she remained locked in the tiny space. She could feel a charley horse building up in her left hamstring. She diverted her thoughts from it and focused on being as still as possible.

A beam of light flickered through the trees. Kate's stomach turned as she realized he was sweeping the area with a flashlight, looking for where they might be hiding. Kate pressed herself back into the nook, pulling Ariel with her, the ferns barely concealing them.

The light passed over their shelter.

Her leg began to quiver with the agony of the muscle cramp. Kate clenched her teeth together as she forced herself not to respond to the urgent pain.

The flashlight beam missed the overhang by mere inches.

Kate thought her heart would completely stop before the light moved on.

She didn't dare move. She was afraid to even think, certain that he'd somehow pick up on it. Her hamstring was now a tight, aching mass of torment. Tears rolled down her cheeks as more and more of her leg became engulfed in the cramp.

She focused on silently controlling her breathing. In... out... slow... quiet. He wouldn't have taken kindly to their escape.

Logan's muttering grew faint, his steps retreating.

He was moving toward Mr. Slocum's, she realized, her stomach twisting. He was betting they'd show up there. For now, they'd bought time, but they couldn't stay here forever. It was cold, they were exhausted, and the risk of another bear loomed. The hiding place was too small for them to spend the night and still be functional tomorrow.

Finally, he seemed far enough away for Kate to risk stretching her leg. The entire back of her thigh was contracted, rock hard, and she rubbed it, trying to relieve the pain without leaving their hiding place. She flexed her foot and moved her leg back and forth.

Mercifully, the cramp began to ease, but it left behind a dull, throbbing ache that Kate knew she'd feel for days to come.

"We'll wait a little bit longer," Kate whispered directly into her daughter's ear, her voice steady for Ariel's sake. "Then we'll figure out what to do next. Maybe we circle around and head for the old logging road instead. Maybe we... I just don't know."

Ariel squeezed her hand. "We're gonna be out like trout," she whispered back.

"Toodledoo, kangaroo."

"Gotta skadoodle, wild pink poodle."

Kate giggled softly, her heart swelling with love. She fought off a new round of tears. She was officially scared—terrified was more like it—and she didn't know what to do.

She truly didn't want to harm Logan or anybody else, but if it came down to him or them, it was definitely going to be him.

Kate's mind raced, looking for solutions that just weren't there. What should she do? Dawn was still many hours away. The nook was hidden, but was it hidden enough? Was anywhere on this mountain safe with Logan prowling around?

"He's not going to give up, is he?" Ariel broke into Kate's Ozzy-official Crazy Train of Thought.

"No," Kate replied bluntly, her voice low. "But neither are we."

She squeezed Ariel in a tight, one-armed hug and kissed the top of her head.

Logan's ghost haunted her. Even though he wasn't there right now, he loomed over them like a cloud covering the moon. She shook it off. That kind of thinking was not going to help them one bit.

She listened carefully and didn't hear anything that sounded human. She awkwardly crawled out and stood up, stretching her leg painfully to relieve the muscles that had cramped so agonizingly. It brought on a new spate of pain that left her holding on to a young sapling for support as she stretched through it. Ariel watched without interrupting.

Finally, the intense pain subsided again. Kate bent from side to side, loosening up her back, then stretched her arms toward the heavens.

What should they do? She hated feeling so indecisive, but fleeing from a crazy, violent ex-boyfriend through the forest was a new experience.

Run TO safety. The words echoed in her head again.

The safest place for them would be with Mr. Slocum. It didn't matter if Logan was expecting them to go there. They could hike around and approach the cabin from the other side.

Once they joined forces with their neighbor, she felt certain that they would be safe. They'd call the police from his landline, and he'd make them what he called his "world-famous cocoa," which was really just an envelope of Swiss Miss with a Hershey's square melting in the bottom. Suddenly, nothing sounded better than being in Mr. Slocum's small, cozy kitchen, sipping that hot beverage from one of his many random mugs.

"What do you say we head to Mr. Slocum's now?" she asked her daughter softly.

"Let's do it," agreed Ariel, her voice still shaky from the near miss with Logan.

She paused to orient them, the North Star faint through the clouds but steady and, somehow, comforting.

"We're going north to get around to the other side of the cabin."

Kate pointed to Polaris. "Remember what I showed you?"

Ariel nodded, scanning the sky.

"You'll never be lost if you can read the stars," Kate reminded the girl, summoning up her dwindling energy for the hike.

Reluctantly, she picked up her backpack and put it on. Ariel followed suit. The Glock went back in the holster, and she picked up her hiking poles. She was ready for this entire situation to be over.

They moved as silently as they could through the dark forest.

To avoid noise, Kate guided them to patches of moss or pine needles, testing each step with her toes for anything that might make a sound when she put her foot down.

Kate used the forest's ambient sounds, such as the creek's trickle, to gauge distance and direction. "If the creek gets louder, we're off course," she whispered to Ariel. "Keep it faint behind us."

Those sounds could also be used when it wasn't possible to mask their steps. They opted to go parallel to the trail, sticking to the shadows.

They'd hiked for about twenty minutes when Kate froze, her hand gripping Ariel's arm. A glint had caught her eye from the trail—something shiny that didn't belong here. "Stay here," she hissed in a whisper.

As Ariel remained where she was, Kate approached the shiny thing as cautiously as she would have if it were a live cobra that had gotten misplaced in North Carolina.

A thin wire stretched across the trail, nearly invisible in the dark. If the moonlight hadn't exposed the metallic thread, they'd have never known it was there.

The tripwire was crude but deliberate, tied to a stick rigged to fall and make noise. It had to be Logan's work—a trap to alert him if they passed.

And if that was the case, he was probably very close.

Her stomach twisted. He was playing games with them, turning the forest into his hunting ground. Worse still, a piece of paper was pinned to a tree with a pocketknife. Kate looked at it with apprehension.

She risked a couple of silent steps closer to see what was on the paper. Her heart sank as she recognized it.

It was a photo of her, Logan, and Ariel, taken years ago when they'd gone on a carefree boating trip. They were laughing, the wind tousling their hair, arms around each other. They looked like a happy little family. Now, the photo was suspended there, crumpled and stained.

"He's been here," Ariel whispered, her voice cracking.

"He's trying to scare us," Kate whispered in reply. "It means he's guessing, not tracking. We're smarter." She left the photo and the tripwire where they were. There was no point in making it obvious that they had been there.

"We keep going," she whispered, her mouth against Ariel's ear. "We just avoid getting directly onto the trail, and we watch for more booby traps."

They headed down the steep hillside, Kate reminding Ariel to use the "handrails" with her free hand—natural features like vines, branches, and rock overhangs. "Be gentle," she clarified. "Just for balance—don't put all your weight on them."

They picked their way down the precarious hillside carefully, avoiding the loose shale and heavy roots that obstructed their path. Every rustle—a squirrel, an owl asking its eternal question, a branch cracking in the distance—made her heart race.

It seemed like hours before they reached a small glen surrounded by dense vines and shrubs. They stopped for a water break, and Kate finally buried the thrice-damned M&M wrappers.

"We're invisible here," she whispered, pulling Ariel close for warmth. "Have a drink and something to eat."

Ariel nodded, her eyes distant. Kate recognized that look. "You okay, Ari?" she asked softly.

Ariel swallowed, her voice small. "That picture... It's like he still thinks he is part of us, that we're his family."

"He isn't," Kate told her fiercely. "You're mine, and I'm yours, and we are a complete family, just us. This is not his mountain. It's ours."

She compulsively checked the Glock. There was definitely still one in the chamber.

A distant snap echoed through the ravine, too heavy for a deer. Kate's grip on the firearm tightened. There were no more alarming noises, and their breathing slowed.

"Let's go," she said to Ariel with a cheer she didn't feel. "We're burning moonlight."

Ariel got up and stiffened her shoulders.

Mother and daughter marched through the forest like they owned it.

They had a major advantage. Logan thought he'd disarmed them back at the cabin. He had no idea about the cache.

Kate knew that this wouldn't end until he was back in prison.

Or until she was forced to use her gun.

Whichever came first was okay with her.

Chapter 21

Ariel needed rest, and so did Kate. She couldn't fight off Logan if she was woozy from lack of sleep, and exhaustion had a way of making bad decisions feel reasonable.

They squeezed into a small, dense thicket and pulled a green-and-brown tarp over themselves to help them blend into the forest, careful to tuck in the edges so metal grommets didn't catch the light.

She was just going to take a little power nap...

...

The first rays of dawn seeped into the thicket. Kate's eyes snapped open, her heart lurching. She woke with her teeth already clenched and her heart pounding a warning — a habit drilled into her by too many mornings that started wrong. She was determined that this would be the last morning that she did so.

Ariel stirred beside her, but didn't awaken. Her taser was clutched in her hand while she slept, knuckles pale with tension even in rest. The forest was waking, a chorus of birdsong mingling with the creek's faint gurgle, but every rustle made her jump and ask herself, Was that Logan?

Kate checked the Glock again. One in the chamber, she chanted in her head. They were safe for now, but their current location was no fortress. Logan's tripwire and that boating photo proved he was hunting way too close for comfort.

"Wakey, wakey," Kate whispered as she shook Ariel lightly.

"Where are my eggs and bakey?" Ariel asked with a sleepy smile.

"We need to move again," Kate whispered, her voice low to avoid carrying. "Dawn gives us light, but it helps him, too. I'm hoping he got tired and went back to our place for a nap, or convinced himself we were headed somewhere else."

Ariel nodded, the smile leaving her face as she remembered the grim reality of their situation. "Where are we headed?" she asked, her voice steady despite the tremor in her hands.

"We're going to Mr. Slocum's," Kate said. "We'll stake it out first, make sure Logan isn't there. But we need help. We can't just keep running around the forest forever."

They crawled from the thicket the same way they'd come in. Kate rolled up the tarp and put it back into her backpack. It was damp with dew, but there was no time to dry it off. The Blue Ridge air was crisp, heavy with fog that clung to the hemlock and rhododendron, making the forest feel like a mythical labyrinth. Even in the stress of the moment, Kate couldn't help but be awed by the storybook beauty of this mountain. She led them onto a mossy path to avoid leaving footprints, her trekking pole probing for slick rocks.

The double-peaked ridge loomed closer, its silhouette a faint guide against the pinkening sky, but the dense Blue Ridge forest, choked with hemlock, rhododendron, and slick shale, hid the ground's dangers. Kate paused, crouching low to avoid casting shadows that Logan's flashlight might catch. Ariel mirrored her.

Kate leaned close, her whisper barely audible. "Remember when I taught you about terrain association? It's like building a map in your head." She pointed to the double-peaked ridge, distinct despite the fog. "You see that ridge with the two humps? It's our anchor. The Slocum place is just below that ridge."

She continued, keeping her voice calm and instructional on purpose. "You pick landmarks—boulders, unusual trees—and use them to keep going in the right direction.

"If you know the mountain's secrets, you don't need a compass. Things like a twisted tree stump or a boulder split like a heart, and you've got a marker."

Ariel nodded, her eyes tracing the ridge, then dropping to a dead, gnarled oak just ahead of them. Its barren branches clawed the sky in a bizarrely beautiful pattern. "Like that tree?" she whispered, pointing.

"Exactly like that tree," Kate said, pride flickering. "Memorize it, then find the next one. We've got this."

She taught Ariel to move in a zigzag pattern, now purposely stepping on rocks or fallen logs to break their trail.

The double-peaked ridge loomed closer, a landmark guiding them through the fog. Kate's ears strained for Logan's boots or voice when a sudden crash stopped her in her tracks.

A doe, startled by their approach, bolted through the underbrush and leapt across the trail in front of them, hooves thundering.

Ariel flinched but suppressed the scream climbing up her throat. Kate gripped her arm. "Just a deer," she whispered calmly, though she felt anything but serene. She could barely hear anything over the panicked thudding of her heart. She took a few calming breaths, and they continued their trek.

When they reached the outcrop, Kate's blood ran cold. Scratched into a birch tree, still fresh with sap, were the words "FAMILY." The carving was crude, Logan's work, his knife marks deep and angry. Nearby, a braided friendship bracelet lay in the dirt. It had been Ariel's, from years ago, one he'd stolen from her. A small pile of cigarette butts lay on the ground. He'd hovered here, watching for them, lying in wait here for quite a while, staking out Mr. Slocum's house, waiting for them to arrive.

Kate touched the pile of butts—they were cold. He'd been here a few hours ago, not recently, which was a relief. He was trying to anticipate their moves, circling like a wolf. He clearly knew they were headed to get help from Mr. Slocum, and he must be furious that they had eluded him so far.

Ariel's breath caught, her eyes locked on the bracelet, her voice barely a whisper. "He kept it... all this time?"

Kate's hand tightened on the Glock, rage battling fear. "He's playing with us," she said, her voice low and fierce. "But we're not his family. We are still going to Mr. Slocum's, but we need to watch the place for a little while to make sure he's not waiting to ambush us. Let's keep walking until we get closer."

Ariel nodded wordlessly. The bracelet had shaken her. They carried on in silence, Kate searching for the right words to comfort her daughter and falling short.

Finally, they reached the double-peaked ridge that was right above the Slocum place. Below the ridge, a narrow gully snaked through a tight thicket, its entrance hidden by a fallen pine. It was a tough descent, but once they were in, they were nearly invisible. It was a perfect hideout to scope out the cabin of their neighbor.

They inched down carefully and ducked into the gully, where everything felt damp. Kate led the way, crawling under a fallen pine. She peered through the brush. She could see the side door, the one that Mr. Slocum always used, and the driveway of the little cabin. They were far enough in not to be spotted by a casual glance. They sat. It seemed like a good place for them to lie in wait for a change.

"We stay here and watch the house for a while," Kate whispered, pulling Ariel close. She knew from her daughter's vacant stare that she was reliving a terrible time, and she made a silent vow that this would end soon—one way or another.

Chapter 22

Ariel's knees were getting damp from the moist dirt of the gully, and the taser felt heavy in her hand. She'd been clutching it so hard that it made her fingers ache. Logan had kept the bracelet for all these years—her favorite bracelet, the one she'd braided with pink and blue thread at summer camp. That stupid carving on the tree, FAMILY, made her stomach twist, like she might puke.

She stared at the ferns absently, and her brain yanked her back. Back to when she was ten years old.

Back to the day when everything went wrong.

...

> The school office smelled like pencil shavings and Mrs. Carter's gross coffee. Ariel sat on the hard chair, swinging her sneakers, her backpack heavy with math homework. The clock ticked too loud: TICK. TICK. TICK. Like it was annoyed with her.
>
> She'd been called out of social studies, right in the middle of a boring lecture about some map. The secretary, Mrs. Carter, had said, "Logan's here for your dentist appointment, sweetie."
>
> Logan? Ariel's tummy flipped. She didn't know she had a dentist appointment. Mom always picked her up for the dentist, bringing her favorite grape

gum to chew after. But Mom was at work, and Ariel hadn't seen her since breakfast, and Mom never forgot things like that.

Maybe she'd sent Logan, even though they'd broken up? Ariel clutched her backpack straps, her friendship bracelet—pink and blue, her favorite colors—sliding down her wrist.

Mrs. Carter led her to the front office, where Logan stood, smiling too big, like a cartoon wolf. He wore a flannel shirt. His hair was messy, and his eyes were... weird. Shiny, like he was excited about something secret. Ariel's skin prickled.

Logan had been Mom's boyfriend. They'd broken up yesterday—Mom said he wasn't right for them, and Ariel had agreed. Logan had been weird lately in ways she couldn't put into words. She always felt like he was trying to catch her and her mom lying to him. It was like he spied on them, though she wasn't sure if Mom knew it, too.

But he'd been nice before, bringing her ice cream, joking about her comic books, helping her with homework. She used to like Logan, even love him, before he started being weird.

Why was he here?

"Hey, kiddo," Logan said, his voice all syrupy. "Ready for the dentist? Your mom asked me to grab you."

Ariel frowned. "Mom didn't say anything about a dentist." Her voice came out small, but she stood taller, gripping her backpack. Something felt off, like when she'd forgotten her lines in the school play and everyone stared, waiting for her to mess up.

Logan's bright white smile didn't budge. "Last-minute thing. She got stuck at work. Come on, let's go." He held out his hand, but Ariel didn't take it. Mrs. Carter was already back at her desk, typing, not even looking.

Ariel's brain buzzed. Mom always called the school if plans changed. She didn't think Mom would send Logan, not after their big fight. Mom had tried to hide it when she was crying in the kitchen, but Ariel knew she had been upset. Mom said he was "gone for good."

But Logan was here, and Mrs. Carter seemed fine with it. Maybe it was okay? Her tummy said no, but she didn't know what to do. She was only ten years old, and even though she was now in double digits, she couldn't just run out of the office.

"Okay," Ariel mumbled, following him to the parking lot, her sneakers dragging. His truck was old, rusty, with a dented fender. It smelled like cigarettes and something sour when she climbed in. No grape gum. No Mom.

Her bracelet caught on the seatbelt, and she tugged it free, her fingers shaky.

Logan started the truck, humming a song she didn't know. "You're gonna love this," he said, glancing at her with that shiny-eyed look. "We're gonna be a family, you, me, and your mom. Forever. We worked things out, and everything is going to be okay again."

Ariel's chest got tight, like she couldn't breathe right. Family? Mom had said she didn't want him in their life anymore. Had she really changed her mind that fast? It didn't sound like Mom.

The truck turned left, away from town, away from the dentist's office she'd been to a million times. The road got bumpy, trees crowding in, no houses, no stores.

It was just the forest on either side of the road.

"Where are we going?" Ariel asked, her voice squeaky. "This isn't the way to the dentist."

Logan's hands tightened on the wheel, his smile gone. "Change of plans, kiddo. Somewhere better. You'll see."

Her heart went thump-thump-thump, too loud, like it wanted to jump out. This wasn't right. She wasn't stupid. She knew what a dentist's office looked like, with its shiny tools and boring magazines. They were in town, where people could get to them easily.

This was just trees and dirt roads. Logan wasn't taking her to get her teeth cleaned. He was taking her somewhere else.

Ariel's eyes darted around the truck. A crumpled soda can in the cupholder, a knife handle sticking out from under his seat. Her bracelet felt heavy, like it was yelling at her to do something. She thought of Mom's stories about being brave, like the time they'd hiked and a snake slithered by, and Mom stayed calm, saying, "Just watch it. Don't panic."

Ariel wasn't calm, but she wasn't going to cry either. She was in double digits, after all.

She reached for the door handle, slow, like she was just scratching her leg. Maybe she could jump out if he stopped. But the truck kept moving, faster now, the forest blurring outside.

"Don't do anything dumb, Ariel," Logan said, not looking at her, his voice sharp like a teacher's. "You gotta trust me. We're going to meet your mom and have a little family vacation."

Ariel's throat burned. She didn't trust him. He wasn't family. He was a liar. And she was pretty sure he was crazy, too.

She thought of Mom, probably still at work, not knowing where she was. She would be so worried when school pick-up time arrived and Ariel was nowhere to be found.

Her fingers brushed the bracelet, and she yanked it off, shoving it into her pocket. The truck slowed at a stop sign, and Ariel's heart jumped. It was now or never. She grabbed the door handle, yanked it, but it was locked. Stupid child lock!

Logan's hand shot out, grabbing her wrist, hard. "I said, don't be dumb," he snapped, his face all wrong, like a mask slipping off. His shiny eyes were scary now, not happy.

Ariel kicked at him, her sneaker hitting his leg, but he didn't let go. "Stop it!" she yelled, her voice cracking. "I want my mom!"

Tears stung her eyes, but she blinked them back. She wasn't a baby. She was smart, like Mom said. She had to think.

Logan ignored her kicks and pulled into a gravel lot, a creepy old house in the distance, half-hidden by pines. "We're here," he said, like it was normal.

Ariel's stomach dropped. This wasn't like any vacation place she had ever been. She twisted her wrist, pulling free, and scrambled for the knife under the seat, her fingers grazing it. Logan grabbed her backpack, yanking her back. "You're staying, Ariel," he said, his voice low, mean. "Family stays together."

Ariel's scream stuck in her throat. She wasn't his family. She was Mom's. And Mom would find *her—she always did. She scowled, made her mean-est face to show Logan he'd better not mess with her.*

...

Ariel blinked, back in the gully, her taser shaking in her hand. The bracelet memory stung, like a cut that wouldn't heal.

Logan was out there, still calling her "family," still trying to take her away. But she wasn't ten anymore. She was 14 now, and stronger, tougher, like Mom. The ferns brushed her face, and she gripped the taser tighter, her jaw set.

This time, she knew exactly who he was.

And she knew she wouldn't go quietly.

Chapter 23

Kate crouched beside Ariel in the gully, ferns tickling her neck, her Glock a steady comfort in her holster. Ariel huddled beside her, taser clutched tight, her eyes still distant. Kate's gut twisted—she hated Logan for this, despised him with the fire of a thousand suns for what he'd done to her daughter as much as what he'd done to her.

"We're okay, Ari," Kate whispered, squeezing her daughter's shoulder. "I'm here, and I will not let him take you anywhere. I swear it."

Ariel gave a shaky nod, forcing a grin. "I'm not worried," she lied. "He's probably tripping over his own traps out there." Her voice wobbled, but the spark was there again, that stubborn flicker Kate loved so much.

Kate played along. "Yeah, we'll probably find him hanging upside down by the foot from one of the tripwires he set up."

They both giggled out of the habit of finding each other funny. In truth, neither of them found their situation particularly funny.

We've been running around the forest playing hide-and-seek for way too long, Kate thought, *and I'm sick of it.*

She scanned the cabin below. Mr. Slocum's place sat quietly in the misty morning. Was it a little too quiet?

She could see that the lights were on, indicating that Mr. Slocum was home and awake, but the fog had shrouded it so thoroughly that she found herself squinting and peering to get a clearer look, to no avail.

And that side door still hung open, swaying and squeaking, like it'd been left in a hurry.

Something felt wrong, but she couldn't tell if her imagination was running away with her or if a genuine threat existed in the cabin. Logan could be waiting, his knife ready, that wild look in his eyes.

"Stay low," Kate murmured. "We are moving up a little closer."

Ariel nodded. They inched along the gully, keeping the cabin in sight, their trekking poles probing for slick shale or Logan's tripwires. Their boots crushed pine needles and autumn leaves, releasing bursts of earthy perfume with each silent step. The forest seemed to bleed its scents—resin, moss, and damp soil—as if the plants were warning each other of the intruders passing through their silent world.

They crept forward, and Kate's mind churned—that open door felt like a trap, but Mr. Slocum was notoriously hard of hearing.

They couldn't run forever, Kate thought, in an effort to convince herself that going to Mr. Slocum's place was the right move.

A snap echoed behind them, sharp, like a twig underfoot. Kate dropped to a crouch, yanking Ariel down with her. "Quiet," she hissed, her heart booming so loudly in her chest that she could no longer hear the other morning noises of the forest. Had that been Logan? Or was it just a deer?

Kate was disoriented. Her heart thundered, drowning out the forest, and she couldn't see through the fog. She waited, and there was no other indication that they were being followed. Her eyes locked on the cabin, still eerily still, the door swaying in the breeze. The whole scenario was like something in a horror movie, but for the life of her, she couldn't figure out how the plucky heroines would come out on top in such a film.

Ariel clutched her taser. She was pale, her eyes dark and wide, her jaw clenched.

Kate had to get a hold of herself. As if Ariel wasn't traumatized enough by this particular jaunt through the forest. She took a deep, steadying breath.

Kate made her decision. They were going to Mr. Slocum's. Now it wasn't just about getting help. They needed to make sure he was okay.

If Logan had hurt that dear man—she stopped herself before she completed the thought.

Kate's boots crunched on the rocky path, Glock drawn, low and ready. Mist painted the Appalachian landscape in purples and grays, fog curling through hemlock and rhododendron like a ghost. Mornings like this made you believe that the legends about these mountains being haunted were true. She quickly banished those thoughts, too. There was no sense in worrying about problems of the supernatural world when they had a giant living problem following them around the mountain.

Ariel stuck close, her breath quick but steady.

That damned door, the screen door squeaking in the breeze, made Kate's stomach churn.

She absolutely knew something was wrong. She felt like she was headed into a trap, but couldn't think of any way to avoid it. Mr. Slocum needed them.

"We're checking on Mr. Slocum," Kate whispered, her voice sharp. "No more games, Ari. Stay right behind me."

Ariel nodded, eyes fierce despite shaky hands holding her taser. "If that creep's there, I'm zapping him into next week," she muttered, trying to make a joke of it, though she was completely serious about her intentions.

They moved low, stepping carefully to avoid making a noise that could alert the stalker to their presence. Kate's trekking pole probed for tripwires or any other surprises Logan might have for them.

Once she had ascertained that the gravel path to the cabin door was clear of hazards, she forced herself to stride forward to the cabin with a confidence she didn't feel. Ariel was close on her heels and took a page from her mother's book, straightening her spine and holding her head high.

Kate felt a little better with her improved posture. Even if Logan was lying in wait, there was no sense in looking like you'd already been whipped. Let Logan be concerned by their lack of visible fear, she thought.

They made it across part of the yard and driveway, and now Mr. Slocum's side door was right in front of them.

Only the screen door was open, swinging in the morning breeze on squeaky hinges. She'd have to remember to let Mr. S. know that his hinges needed to be oiled, Kate thought, like it was just an ordinary visit.

She paused before reaching out to knock loudly on the door. The loud noise made Ariel jump, and worried Kate. It might lure Logan straight to their location. But they couldn't exactly walk right into the neighbor's cabin unannounced, or Logan wouldn't be their biggest problem. Walking into someone's house uninvited around these parts was a good way to end up being welcomed with a shotgun full of buckshot.

There was no answer. She strained to hear if there were any signs that Mr. Slocum was inside the cabin and awake. It was silent inside. The only sign he was definitely here was that his truck was in the driveway.

Kate reached for the doorknob, her stomach churning with such dread that she felt ill. As she touched the cool brass of the doorknob, she couldn't hear a thing over the sound of her blood rushing in her ears, pounding in time with her heart. She drew a shaky breath and twisted the knob, half hoping to find it locked so that she could say she had tried but couldn't get in.

However, the knob turned easily under her hand, and the door swung open into the familiar, cluttered kitchen. Kate pushed it all the way back to ensure that Logan wasn't behind it, waiting to jump them the moment they were both inside.

The kitchen was small, and the light over the sink was on, showing that the room was clear of any presence that shouldn't be there. Kate pushed the door shut with her rear while keeping her eyes fixed on the dark rooms beyond the kitchen. She reached back, felt for the knob, and locked the door so nobody could come in behind them without making a lot of noise. Ariel was at her left hand, looking around the cozy room.

A mug of coffee sat on the counter beside a spoon. Kate touched the mug, hoping it would still be hot. It wasn't. The blue earthenware was chilly under her fingertips. It had been sitting there for a while. Kate's heart dropped. That wasn't a great sign. Mr. Slocum was adamant about having his two cups of Folger's Instant coffee every morning. He loved the stuff, drinking it black. In Kate's opinion, it tasted awful, like a cup of tar. She remembered the first time she had accepted a cup of coffee from her neighbor and had tried to pretend like it was great—

Wait...

She needed to focus on the rooms beyond the kitchen. While the memories were far more pleasant, she had a job at hand.

"Mr. Slocum?" she called out loudly, in deference to her neighbor's hearing problems. "It's Kate and Ariel from next door. Mr. Slocum?"

There was no reply. The house felt empty, echoing, unfamiliar.

Next, she turned to the landline phone, which was hanging on the kitchen wall. An old phone book was in a basket hanging below it. She picked up the receiver and put it to her ear. She pushed the buttons frantically, trying to get a dial tone.

Ariel had followed the cord to where it plugged into the wall. Not only was the cord cut, but the jack had also been pulled out of the wall, leaving the raw ends of the wires exposed.

Kate flinched at the sight of it. Okay, no calling the police, she thought.

She accepted the unpleasant fact that she was going to have to search the cabin.

"Ariel, you are waiting in the kitchen," she told her daughter firmly. As Ariel's mouth opened to express her displeasure, Kate cut her off. "That isn't a question. It's a statement. You are waiting here to stand watch. Warn me if you see Logan, okay?"

Ariel didn't look happy, but she nodded brusquely, accepting her assignment.

Kate fought through the dread that swamped her and took her first step out of the kitchen, Glock taking the lead as she proceeded to clear the next room.

Chapter 24

Kate cautiously entered the next room, back against the wall to protect herself.

The living room smelled comforting, the familiar scent of damp wool and a toasty fire. Mr. Slocum always kept a fire going in the woodstove the moment it got chilly enough, but today, the ashes inside the cast-iron stove were cold.

Kate's eyes swept the space. It looked normal. She felt hopeful when she saw his recliner, the crocheted blanket his late wife had made draped neatly over the back. A half-finished jigsaw puzzle of a barn owl was spread across the coffee table.

Nothing overturned, nothing broken.

No signs of struggle.

It was just still.

Too still.

She took a quick look behind the sofa, which was the only possible hiding place in the small room. Nothing.

Her boots whispered over the old braided rug as she moved toward the hallway.

"Mr. Slocum?" she called again, louder this time. *I don't want to stumble upon the old man if he's still in bed or—heaven forbid—in the shower—how embarrassing for both of us,* she thought.

Her voice sounded strange in the silent cabin. It was too sharp, too alive.

She waited hopefully for a response.

Prayed for a response.

There was no answer.

She moved into the hallway and switched on the light. Only one bulb burned weakly overhead. She was going to check each room, with Mr. Slocum's room being the last.

The first door on the right led to the guest room. She checked under the empty bed, sheets tight and crisp. She looked in the closet and was greeted by the faint scent of mothballs.

The bathroom door was open, and the shower curtain was pulled aside, revealing an empty tub and neatly hung towels. No one there, nothing out of place.

There was only one room left. Her feet felt heavy as she trudged toward the last door. "Mr. Slocum?" she called again, hopefully waiting for an answer.

The door was almost closed—opened just a crack.

She hesitated, closing her eyes for a moment. She knocked on the bedroom door, hoping that he was in bed, taking a nap, and that this had all been a silly leap of her imagination.

Again, there was no answer.

She eased the door open with the muzzle of her Glock. The hinges gave a slight creak, high-pitched. She was betting Mr. Slocum was unable to hear it; otherwise, he would have oiled the offending hardware immediately.

The scent hit her firs. It smelled of iron and something faintly metallic and sweet, undercut by shaving soap. She closed her eyes and whispered an unintelligible prayer.

Her brain refused to name the scent until she saw him.

Mr. Slocum sat in his chair beside the window, facing the mountains. His hands rested neatly on his knees, palms up, like he'd been waiting for something. He wore his favorite flannel shirt. A wilted sunflower had been tucked into the breast pocket. There was something dark on his shirt.

Kate's throat constricted. "Oh, no. Oh, Mr. S..."

She stepped closer. The chair creaked as her boot brushed it. Mr. Slocum didn't move. His head lolled slightly to one side, and she saw the neat slice across his throat. The blood had soaked one side of his gray-and-blue plaid shirt, coloring over the pattern.

"No," Kate said again, this time more firmly, as if she could make this horrible event be erased by sheer strength of will.

Then she noticed the reddish-brown smudges on his bedroom wall.

Words, her brain registered numbly, without actually reading them.

They had not been put on the wall with paint. They'd been written in Mr. Slocum's blood.

The words had been written in a large, uneven scrawl. Thick, dark strokes gleamed in the weak light from the window, almost seeming moist.

FAMILY IS FOREVER.

When she read the words, her hand began to tremble so badly she almost dropped the gun.

Ariel's voice floated from the kitchen. "Mom? You okay?"

Kate swallowed hard and forced her voice steady. It came out broken anyway. "Stay where you are, baby."

She crouched beside the chair, two fingers to the side of his neck, hoping to find a pulse, knowing she wouldn't. He was cold. Strangely, the skin was softer than she would have expected from a corpse, she noted, then squelched the hysterical thought.

The pulse was gone. He was dead, and this hadn't just happened.

Logan had been here earlier.

Waiting.

Setting the trap.

Her vision tunneled. The edges of the room went gray. She forced herself to breathe through her nose, slow, steady, like she'd taught Ariel. Counting, breathing, clearing her mind.

In for four.

Hold for four.

Out for four.

The dizziness began to subside when a creak from a floorboard in the hallway pulled her out of her quick meditation. Someone was in the hall behind her.

Kate whirled around, gun raised, eye staring down the front sight. When she saw it was her daughter, she immediately pointed the gun toward the floor and holstered it.

"I said to stay in the kitchen!"

But the girl was already in the doorway, hand to her mouth, eyes wide.

"Oh no," she whispered. "Is he—dead?"

Kate rose, senses suddenly sharp and back in control. She caught her daughter by the shoulders, turning her toward the door. "Don't look, sweetheart. Look at me."

Ariel's eyes filled with tears, but she disobeyed, turning back to the gruesome scene. "He wrote that, didn't he? Logan did?"

Kate didn't answer. She didn't have to. She gently pushed the girl from the room and quietly closed the door behind them. She guided Ariel back toward the kitchen. "Sit down. I'll make you some tea."

Ariel nodded, wiping her nose on her sleeve as she perched on the old red vinyl kitchen chair. Soon, the kettle was bubbling merrily on the stove. Kate opened a cabinet, where she knew her friend had kept the tea, and that simple thought made her eyes fill with tears again. Everything in this kitchen was so normal, and nothing about this morning was.

"Mom, what are we going to do?" Ariel asked, eyes reddened with unshed tears. Kate set the mug of tea in front of Ariel and watched the steam curl between them, carrying the scent of mint and metal.

Kate looked toward the hook where Mr. Slocum kept the keys to his beautifully maintained 1971 Dodge Ram. The keys were gone.

"Wait here," she ordered Ariel. "I mean it. You hear me this time?"

Ariel nodded wordlessly, tears slipping from her eyes.

Full of dread, Kate trudged reluctantly back down the dark hallway to Mr. Slocum's room. He was, of course, exactly how she had left him.

"I'm sorry to do this," she whispered apologetically, even though Mr. Slocum was far beyond hearing the words. She patted his pockets, searching for the keys. His body was stiff and unyielding. She felt something promising in his right pants pocket. Shuddering at her proximity to a dead man, she leaned across him to reach into the pocket.

Victoriously, she pulled out a set of keys. Finally, something had gone right, and they could get the heck out of there and let the police handle things. "Thank you, my friend," she said to Mr. Slocum as if he could hear her.

When she strode back through the kitchen, she had a feeling of elation. She was not going to be a victim. She would save herself and save her daughter and let the cops do their jobs.

She dangled the keys in front of Ariel. "Look—I found Mr. Slocum's truck keys!"

Ariel perked up at the sight of the keys. She, too, fervently wanted to get out of there.

"Gather up our stuff while I go start the truck," Kate told her daughter, then she walked outside with purpose. This was finally going to be over. It had to be.

She got into the old truck. The leather seats were so old and well-worn that they felt as soft as fabric to the touch. Kate put the key into the ignition.

Click. Click. Click.

"No, no, NO!" Kate cried, trying the key again.

Her efforts were met with nothing but dead clicks. Just like her own Jeep, the truck had been sabotaged. It was not going to start.

Ariel was standing on the back stoop, the one where the door had been swinging in the breeze. "He got to it, didn't he?" she asked flatly. Her voice seemed resigned and oddly adult.

Kate nodded, unable to find the right words. She pounded on the driver's side window with the flat of her hands and screamed, "DAMMIT!" She hammered her hands against the steering wheel, ineffectually.

She got out of the truck and threw the useless keys as hard as she could toward the house. She slammed the truck door shut with both hands as hard as she could.

She took some deep breaths, willing herself to calm down. Her hands hurt from where she'd struck the steering wheel.

"He's never going to stop." Ariel had appeared at her side, holding both backpacks, eerily calm during her mother's display of anger. "Nowhere is safe for us, not even Haven Hill."

Kate looked at her daughter—pale, precious, trying to be brave—and knew that they could not keep running.

"You're right," Kate replied. "He's never going to stop. Not until we stop him."

Her hands were steady now, unnaturally so, and that scared her a little. Somewhere between the bedroom and this moment, something in her had gone quiet. The shaking had stopped. The fear settled into hardness inside her chest.

Mr. Slocum's blood had written the truth on the wall for her, too.

Family is forever.

Fine.

She would protect hers forever, too—even if it meant using all her training in a way she had never intended. She unconsciously flexed her fingers, as if remembering the weight of her weapon.

She went back inside the house of her dear friend.

Kate carefully checked that the stove was off and all the lamps were turned off to prevent a possible fire. Then, for what felt like the very last time, she closed Mr. Slocum's door behind her and locked it with the spare key, which she put back in its hiding place.

It felt wrong to leave him there alone. But he cared for them and would want them to be safe.

They had to go.

Chapter 25

Kate was so shaken she didn't remember leaving the cup in the sink or locking the cabin door behind them, but somehow they were back outside in the dusky light, mist clinging to their hair, the mountain utterly still. Even the birds were eerily quiet.

The air smelled of rain. She took one last look at the truck, the half-open door, then turned Ariel toward the trail.

"We're going home."

The walk back to Haven Hill was silent except for their boots crunching through wet leaves. Ariel carried her pack like a soldier, eyes straight ahead. No questions, no jokes. Just the quiet weight of grief and understanding between them.

By the time the metal roof of their own cabin came into view, the fog had lifted just enough to clearly reveal it.

But the cabin wasn't the only thing she could see clearly. She also knew what had to be done, and she was fully prepared to do it. Kate felt the shift inside her, the way she sometimes felt the weather changing in her bones.

The front door had been left unlocked.

Inside, she cleared each room again: great room, bedrooms, behind the shower curtain, and in the kitchen.

Kate had to choke back a hysterical giggle when she mused that she should contact the purveyors of that room-clearing course and give them a bonus, considering how many times she had used those techniques in the past 48 hours alone.

She was not going back down into the basement. There was no way to keep that room secure because of the window they had broken when they made their earlier escape. Kate put the Molly bar in place across the basement door, and together, they pushed the heavy kitchen table back in front of it for added security.

The cabin was empty of threats. Logan wasn't there.

They were safe.

For now.

Quickly, Kate built a small fire in the woodstove to take the autumn chill off the cabin, the snap of kindling loud in the quiet room.

"I don't know about you, but I am desperate for a shower," she said to Ariel, surprised by that perfectly normal urge in this anything-but-normal situation.

"SAME," Ariel agreed, dramatically sniffing her armpits and making a disgusted face.

Kate smiled, the expression on her face catching her by surprise. It was crazy how a world this normal could exist alongside a world where her deranged ex-boyfriend was stalking them in the Appalachian forest.

"Let's take turns standing watch. I want you to move from window to window, looking outside. But stay behind the wall and glance out the windows at an angle so you aren't giving Logan a clear view," she explained. "Got it? Show me."

Ariel sidled along the wall and stood beside the window, her back to the room, looking out toward one side of the yard. Then, getting low, she crouched under the window to make her way to the other side for a different angle.

Kate nodded in approval. "Change one thing. Put your back against the wall of the cabin. It gives you a smaller profile."

"Aye, aye, captain." Ariel saluted her smartly.

Kate turned her Glock around to give it butt first to Ariel. She paused before extending the firearm. The weight of the gun was nothing compared to the emotional weight of what she was about to instruct Ariel to do. "If he comes through that door, shoot him. Keep shooting until he is down and not getting back up. You have no option. It's self-defense, do you understand me?"

Ariel nodded solemnly, and reluctantly, Kate handed her the gun.

Kate grabbed some clean clothes from her room, then hurried into the bathroom, eager to wash off the grime of the past two days. She stripped off her clothes while the water was getting hot. The pile of dirty laundry was stained, telling a story—dirt, leaves, sweat, and blood.

The moment the hot water hit her, Kate surprised herself by starting to cry. The tears flowed as she sobbed silently. She slid down to sit on the floor of the bathtub while the water from the showerhead pelted her. After a few minutes, the tears passed. She scrubbed herself from head to toe with fresh-smelling soap and a pink pouf, then washed and conditioned her hair. What a weird thing to do, she thought, but it was habits taking control of a body and brain that had been through too much.

She stood for a final rinse, then stepped out of the shower and put on her fresh clothing. She'd chosen cozy black sweatpants, underwear, a comfy sports bra, and a long-sleeved black t-shirt. She wanted something she could wear napping on the couch or wandering through the woods, and this solemn ensemble fit the bill.

While Ariel showered, Kate kept watch. She combed out her hair and put it in two tight French braids that she clipped together in the back and rolled under for a tight, no-nonsense hairstyle with nothing to grab.

Ariel rejoined her, clean and fresh smelling. "You look like a commando chick from a movie," she observed.

Kate smiled, though it didn't quite reach her eyes. "I guess movies are right about some things."

"Are you hungry? I can make some sandwiches," Ariel offered.

Kate hadn't been hungry until she thought about sinking her teeth into a roast beef and Swiss cheese sandwich, but suddenly she was ravenous. While Ariel made the sandwiches, she pushed the heavy armoire in front of the door again and secured the doors to the bedrooms. It was easier, she had learned, to defend just one room.

They ate at the kitchen table without a word, gobbling down the food like they had been starved for weeks. Wordlessly, Ariel made a second round of sandwiches, which they polished off at a more leisurely pace.

Once she had eaten the last crumb from her paper plate, Kate pushed her chair back from the table and stretched her arms over her head. The big stretch felt good after the past two days of hiding in the forest and making herself as small as possible.

"I have to go downstairs and get a few supplies. Can you keep watch up here?"

Ariel nodded and helped Kate move the heavy kitchen table away from the basement door. Kate knew exactly what she needed and returned in a flash with a plastic tub labeled "XMAS" and a couple of spools of fishing line on top of it. Ariel looked at her curiously as they moved the big table back into place in front of the basement door, legs shrieking across the kitchen floor. Then they stacked the dining chairs to form a barricade in front of the back door.

"We're going to set a perimeter so we don't have to watch quite as closely," Kate explained. "I need you out there with the other gun while I put this up." She put her own Glock into a holster and handed an additional holster to Ariel.

They moved the heavy armoire together and went outside, cautiously looking around before stepping off the porch.

Then Kate started setting up the perimeter. She stretched a fishing line low across the entry paths, threading them with little bells from the Christmas box. At each end, she added a few empty cans from their recycling bin and filled them with pebbles. If Logan were to stumble over one of the tripwires, it would all make a heck of a noise.

"A redneck burglar alarm," proclaimed Ariel. She sat on the porch step, keeping a watchful eye on the forest around them.

Kate forced a laugh, trying to act like she wasn't scared to death.

"Mom?" she asked quietly. "If he comes here, what do we do?"

Kate tied the last knot and pulled the string taut. "We let him know he picked the wrong house."

She debated for a moment whether to install similar alarms at the bottom of the steps leading up to the front and back porches. She decided against it for just one reason: if they had to flee, she didn't want herself or Ariel to be slowed down by tripwires.

She didn't know yet what came after the traps, whether she'd go after him or make him come to her.

Both options were ugly. Leaving Ariel alone felt like standing on the edge of a cliff. Taking her along might be worse. But one thing was certain—she couldn't risk him finding them unprepared again.

She took a deep breath of the cool mountain air, the scent of wet pine and chimney smoke curling into her lungs, and made herself a silent promise:

They would not be victims.

They were drawing Logan in so they could finish this.

Chapter 26

The fire in the woodstove had burned down to coals, just enough to glow behind the grate. Outside, the forest had gone still, that deep-mountain quiet where even the crickets seemed to hold their breath, waiting for... something.

Ariel sat cross-legged on the lavender velvet couch, wrapped in a colorful granny-square blanket Kate had crocheted. Her long, thick hair was still damp from her shower, curling in a halo of little ringlets around her face. The small bells from the fishing-line perimeter jingled faintly whenever the wind shifted, but the cans—the sign the perimeter was breached—were silent.

Kate checked each window once more before settling uneasily into the big leather armchair across from her. She kept her voice low.

"You did good today, kiddo. I know you're scared."

Ariel gave a lopsided shrug. "Scared's not the same as weak, right?"

That earned a thin smile. "No. It isn't." Kate studied her daughter's face—pale under the lamplight but steady. "Tomorrow I'm getting up early to look for his trail. Just far enough to see which direction he's working from."

"You're leaving me here? Alone?" Ariel's voice cracked, then steadied, though it came out higher than normal. She was not on board with the plan. "What if he comes back? What if we don't even make it until tomorrow before he comes back, Mom?"

"He won't tonight," Kate said firmly, though she believed it only halfway. "Tomorrow, if he does, those bells will tell you long before he's close. You grab the Glock, you get behind the refrigerator, and you wait for him to make the first move."

Ariel swallowed. "And then?"

"Then you scream bloody murder and shoot till he stops moving. By then, I'll be on my way back."

The girl nodded, but her eyes glistened. "And what if you don't come back?"

Kate reached across the arm of the leather chair and took her hand. For a breath, she felt the small, private crack of that possibility open inside her, until she slammed it shut and continued speaking with practiced calm. "Then you walk down to the Slocum place in daylight, get onto the ranger road, and keep walking until you hit the first mailbox. Somebody will stop for you."

She paused and stared into her daughter's eyes, willing her to feel the oath in her words. "But I will come back."

They sat in silence for a while, listening to the stove tick and the soft sigh of the wind. Somewhere outside, an owl called.

After a time, Ariel whispered, "Mom?"

"Yes?"

"Do you think he's out there right now? Watching?"

Kate's gaze drifted to the window where the dark pressed against the glass. "Yes," she said quietly. "He probably is. Let him watch out there in the cold while we are warm and cozy in here. Tomorrow we'll make sure he sees exactly what we want him to see."

Ariel's grip tightened. "Promise me one thing?"

"What's that?"

"End this. For good."

Kate didn't answer. She only squeezed her daughter's hand, then stood and added a log on top of the coals, careful to place it just right so it would smolder overnight and keep them warm.

Ariel shifted, then rose and padded to the kitchen, where the refrigerator hunched like a pale sentinel. She ducked behind it and peeked out, testing how she could move from one side to the other without being seen, a small, rehearsed motion that felt ridiculous and brave all at once. Kate watched the practice, a slight shudder at the back of her throat. It was one thing to do these little drills and practice runs in the safety of a course. It was quite another watching Ariel prepare for actual combat.

When Ariel returned to the sofa, Kate joined her, pulling her close in a maternal embrace.

All the while, the bells outside gave soft, nervous chimes that faded into the night.

Chapter 27

When Ariel woke up, her mother was standing at the window, staring out into the forest.

"Good morning, sweet girl." She didn't turn her head away from the window. Mom always knew when she was awake, sometimes, like today, without even looking.

"Morning, Mama," Ariel said sleepily as she padded to the bathroom.

When she emerged, her mom looked serious, the easy warmth of the morning already gone.

"I have an extra pistol for you. I'm trusting you to use good judgment with this."

Ariel nodded soberly as her mother placed the gun in her hand, butt first. It was heavy, but a familiar weight. She'd had lessons, and she and her mom regularly went to a shooting range to keep their skills sharp.

"Keep the door locked behind me. Don't open it for anyone. Not even me, unless I knock twice and say your name."

Ariel hesitated, then stood and wrapped her arms around her mother's waist. "Be careful."

Kate pressed her cheek to the top of Ariel's head, breathing in soap and woodsmoke, holding on for one extra heartbeat. "Always."

When Mom stepped out onto the porch, Ariel duti-fully locked the door behind her and shoved the armoire into place, making it screech across the floor.

Then she stood at the living room window, silent and still, until her mother disappeared into the forest.

...

A faint jingle echoed through the cabin. One of the bells.

Ariel froze, breath caught in her throat. She had taken an older book off the shelf to try to calm herself. She had read The Secret Garden a thousand times, and she could practically recite it, line by line. That beautiful, familiar story, she was sure, would help settle her nerves.

The sound came once, then nothing. She waited, ears straining, counting in her head. Ten seconds. Twenty. Thirty. No follow-up noise—maybe it had been the wind.

She slipped behind the refrigerator, crouched low, gun in hand. The tile floor pressed cold through her socks. She could smell coffee and her mother's soap. It reminded her that Mom was out there, moving through the woods alone, hunting.

She shivered.

She got up from her place behind the refrigerator and put on her boots so her feet would stay warm and she'd be ready.

Ready for what, she wasn't sure. She just knew she'd feel better with her shoes on. Then she took a pillow from the couch, the afghan, and her book, and set up a retreat behind the cover of the refrigerator.

A bulletproof pillow fort, she thought, and almost giggled wildly.

Her heart thudded so loudly she was sure he'd hear it through the walls.

...

She thought back to when she had been taken by Logan.

> On the third day with Logan, Ariel decided to trick him. She pretended to be sick. She coughed and coughed. She attempted to look wan and lethargic. She complained of a bad headache and sore throat. She even cried some to prove how bad she felt.
>
> Logan, of course, did not have any children's cough syrup at the awful cabin he was keeping her in. When he set off to go get more, Ariel sobbed even louder, pretending she was scared to be left behind. She thought about Mom and her room at home. She thought about her Tamagatchi that she had named Amelia, after the famous pilot. She figured Amelia would be dead because nobody would remember to feed her. All of these thoughts helped her bring real tears on display.

So it was no surprise when Logan said she could come with him. He wasn't super nice about it and told her she'd better not make any trouble.

They got into his truck again, Ariel fake-coughing and Logan trying to find something on the radio besides preacher shows.

Finally, they arrived in a town that she didn't recognize. They must have gone the opposite way from home, she thought. When they passed a bus station she stared at it longingly for a moment, then looked down and coughed some more. She didn't want to give away her plan.

When they arrived at the CVS parking lot, Ariel brought herself to tears again. No, she absolutely did not want to go inside with Logan while he bought childrens' cough syrup and tylenol. She just wanted to take a nap in the truck.

Logan got out, taking the keys with him and locking his door behind him. Ariel leaned her head against the passenger window and watched him go inside through her eyelashes.

Once he was in, she opened her eyes all the way and looked at the store. He didn't appear to be near any of the windows. This was her chance.

She scootched across the leather seats over to the driver side door. When she opened it, the alarm erupted since it had been locked from the outside. She froze for only a second, and then she ran.

She ran as fast as she could, all the way down the road they had driven on that had a bus station. She'd never used a bus for transportation aside from the school bus, but she was confident she could figure it out. She ran into the station then visited the bathroom for a minute to catch her breath. She had never run so fast in her entire life.

She splashed some water on her face and sat on a toilet just to rest. Finally, she felt like she was ready to face the world again.

The station was confusing but soon she found that all the stops had signs that lit up with the name of the destinations. She found one for her town and discovered it was aready loading to leave. She was ecstatic that she'd soon see Mom again.

She boarded the bus and politely said hello to the driver. She began to walk past, and he reached his arm out to block her.

"Where's your ticket, Little Missy?"

Ariel hadn't known she'd need a ticket, and now she felt kind of dumb. The tears in her eyes were real this time.

"I'm sorry, I didn't know I needed a ticket, but I have to get home." She began to outright sob, which was embarrassing.

The driver asked how old she was, where her Mom was, and why she was traveling alone. It didn't take him long to figure out that there was something very wrong.

She looked out the window and saw Logan. He was so tall that he stood higher than most of the people at the bus station. And he looked very, very mad. He was so mad his face was red.

"Please don't make me get off the bus," Ariel cried. She felt like she might throw up."I'm afraid my mom's ex-boyfriend will make me go with him."

That was when Logan spotted her. He came up to the bus and asked the driver if he could get his little girl. "I'm NOT his little girl!" Ariel told the driver. "Don't make me go with him!"

The kindly driver patted her arm and promised she could stay on the bus. He told her that he'd wait there with her until the police arrived.

When the police arrived, Logan was nowhere to be seen. The short one looked at his phone and at her. "I think it's her," he said to the taller policeman.

"What's your name, sweetie?" the tall one asked.

"My name is Ariel Lindsey," she replied, proud that she could easily answer his question.

"Oh, honey, your mama has the whole state looking for you!" the short one chimed in.

They told her she was a smart girl. Then they drove her right home to see her Mom, and the very bad adventure with Logan was over...

...

Ariel strained to hear the bells again.

The fire had sunk to embers, and the woodstove's contents glowed faintly orange. She glanced toward the front windows but kept her body angled behind cover. She wanted to add another log to the fire and had just about talked herself into it when she froze again, listening.

The refrigerator clicked, then resumed its low hum, loud in the quiet cabin.

Then—another sound. A single can clinked, sharper this time, followed by the light brush of something against the porch railing.

That was definitely something.

She lifted the Glock with trembling hands and sighted toward the door. "Please be the wind, please be the wind," she whispered over and over, a desperate one-line prayer.

Someone was out there.

Outside, the line of bells shivered once more.

Chapter 28

When Kate awoke, it took her a moment to remember why she'd been asleep on the large leather chair in the living room. She remembered what was really going on quickly, and her brief moment of peaceful confusion was gone.

In the kitchen, she made coffee—her daily ritual. It felt absurd to be doing something so normal when she was heading out to track a man down and might have to kill him. The smell filled the cabin, sharp and bitter, oddly comforting. She went into her bedroom to pull up a loosened floorboard. There lay another Glock 19 with two magazines. She pulled them out and replaced the floorboard.

Outside the windows, dawn was still more shadow than light. The fog lay low, veiling the trees, and every branch glittered with moisture.

Kate scooted the armoire over just a little bit and eased the front door open just wide enough to feel the air on her face. Nothing moved. The perimeter lines were still, the cans untouched. The scent of rain lingered, mingling with the sharp tang of pine and hemlock.

She heard movement behind her and said without turning, "Good morning, sweet girl."

"Morning, Mama," Ariel said sleepily as she padded to the bathroom.

Kate flinched. Her daughter hadn't called her Mama in years. The word reached back to when things were soft and safe—before Logan had entered their lives.

"I'm going to follow his trail while it's still early," Kate said quietly when Ariel emerged from her much-needed shower. "If I'm not back by noon, stay here. Keep the fire low. If you hear the bells—"

Ariel straightened, blinking hard. "I remember. Behind the fridge."

"I have an extra pistol for you. I'm trusting you to use good judgment with this."

Ariel nodded soberly as her mother placed the gun in her hand, butt first.

Pride and guilt twisted together in her chest. This must be what mothers in war zones felt like—teaching their children that someone might be coming to hurt them. Teaching them the difference between cover and concealment. Teaching them that sometimes it wasn't just okay, but necessary, to kill someone.

"Keep the door locked behind me. Don't open it for anyone. Not even me, unless I knock twice and say your name."

Ariel hesitated, then stood and wrapped her arms around her mother's waist. "Be careful."

Kate pressed her cheek to the top of Ariel's head, breathing in soap and woodsmoke. "Always."

It was hard to let go, but finally, Kate stepped onto the porch. The boards were slick with dew, the air cold enough to sting her lungs.

Behind her, the door lock clicked, and the armoire groaned in protest as Ariel pushed the heavy piece into place. Somewhere in the distance, a crow called once—low and harsh, as if warning Kate to be wary of what waited in the forest.

As she crossed the yard, a gust stirred the bells, just a whisper of sound, but it tightened something inside her. She followed the trail down the slope, past the garden gone wild, into the gray hush of the trees.

The forest was damp and gray at this hour of the morning, the mist curling low across the ground like smoke.

Deeper in the forest, a branch cracked, and she froze—it had not been loud enough to be threatening, but just loud enough to remind her that she wasn't alone in these woods.

Behind her, Haven Hill stood sentry. A curl of smoke from the chimney, the faint glimmer of light through the curtains, the shape of her daughter standing in the window, watching until the forest swallowed her mother whole.

Kate moved slowly, every step measured. She wasn't following tracks anymore so much as feeling for them—the tilt of disturbed moss, the faint depression where a boot had pressed through wet leaves.

It felt like she had walked for hours before she saw it.

A cigarette butt gleamed white on the forest floor, near a fallen log, dry and clean of mud. Too new. Too deliberate.

Her pulse quickened. He had wanted her to see this, and it was recent. Why? Was he leading her into a trap?

She crouched, studied it without touching it, then looked up into the fog. The woods were utterly still, so quiet it felt unnatural, like the world had ended and the only thing left alive was her.

Kate straightened, brushing leaves and dirt from her dew-dampened knees. She kept walking.

There—another sign. Her own boot print. Only this time, another track lay on top of it, pressed deep and fresh, toes pointed the opposite direction.

He'd walked her trail backward. Circling. Studying.

He wasn't running from her.

He was stalking her.

A chill ran through her despite the sweat trickling down her spine.

The forest suddenly felt smaller, the air heavy and close. Every branch seemed to lean inward to catch at her clothing. She had the intense feeling that she was being watched, maybe even being trapped, but she couldn't see anyone through the brush.

What on earth had she been thinking? Had she really thought she could go out into the woods and hunt down her ex-boyfriend, who was straight out of jail? That was arrogance, not courage. Maybe she was nuts.

She turned back toward Haven Hill. There had to be a better way to end this.

Kate broke into a jog, hiking boots silent on wet soil. The mist had thinned just enough to show the roofline of Haven Hill through the trees. She paused when she saw it—another cigarette butt. It was like Hansel and Gretel's famous trail of breadcrumbs, except this trail was nicotine-induced.

Finally, she reached the clearing where her beloved cabin stood, a cheerful sentinel in the dappled sunlight.

And there it was—in the mud beside the garden fence—a new footprint, crisp and deep, toes pointed toward the porch.

He was already there. A few cigarette butts indicated that Logan had been there for a while.

"Ariel," she whispered, feeling a wave of devastation wash over her. Her plan had been arrogance dressed as bravery. It had been stupid.

And Ariel might be paying the price.

She raised the pistol and kept moving, each step faster, the weight of the forest pressing at her back.

Chapter 29

Kate stepped out of the treeline with her pistol raised, breath coming fast and tight. Haven Hill shimmered through the thinning fog like a beacon. For one dizzy moment, she felt relief—home, safety, her little girl.

Quickly, quietly, she raced to the porch.

But then she stopped short, feet slipping in the wet gravel.

Her stomach turned to stone.

Bootprints.

Big ones, far too big to be hers or Ariel's.

They were fresh enough that the mud still glistened wetly.

The prints climbed the steps one by one, tracking straight toward the old teal-painted rocking chair that sat in the corner of the porch by the great-room window.

Kate's pulse roared in her ears.

The chair wasn't how she'd left it.

It wasn't looking out toward the wooded view she loved so much.

It was angled slightly toward the glass—toward inside the cabin, where Ariel would have been moving... reading... breathing.

She stepped closer.

Saw something on the porch boards.

A cigarette butt.

Then another.

And then she saw the third—still slightly smoking, a thin wisp curling upward like a taunt. The acrid smell hit her nose: fresh, sharp, unmistakably Logan. He had just been here.

Minutes ago. Maybe seconds.

He had watched her daughter through the glass.

He'd watched for a while—long enough to smoke three cigarettes to the filter.

And he hadn't come empty-handed.

Her throat closed. Air rasped shallowly in her chest.

One of her perimeter bells—cut free, the fishing line still tied to its loop—was sitting neatly on the railing beside the last cigarette butt.

Placed like a gift.

Or a warning.

Or a taunt.

He hadn't just crossed their traps.

He'd dismantled them.

And left a piece on display so she'd know exactly how easily he'd done it.

Kate felt the forest press in behind her, cold and enormous.

"Hold on, baby," she whispered. "Mama's coming."

Then she reached for the doorknob. To her relief, it was still locked tight.

She knocked loudly, twice. "Ariel!"

She had given the signal. She strained to hear movement from inside. It was quiet.

There was nothing but stillness inside the cabin.

She knocked again and called her daughter's name. Her heart began to pound so loudly that she couldn't hear if there was movement in the house or not.

Finally, she heard that precious voice, tenuous but still there.

"Mom?"

"It's me, baby. Let me in."

She lifted her Glock with both hands and turned her back toward the door, sweeping the yard while Ariel pushed the heavy armoire out of the way and unlocked it.

Her heart began hammering again as a single, shattering truth locked into place:

He could have taken Ariel. He could have killed her.

But he didn't.

In his twisted mind, she realized, he wanted her to feel chosen.

He wanted her to feel grateful to him.

The door opened just wide enough to let Kate in. Ariel peeked through the opening, her dark eyes wide in her pale face.

Kate squeezed through, eyes burning.

The familiar smell of woodsmoke, coffee, and Ariel's shampoo hit her all at once.

It should have soothed her.

It nearly brought her to her knees.

Ariel shoved the door shut the second her mother was clear, flipping the locks with shaking fingers. The heavy armoire scraped back into place with a dull grind as they both leaned their weight into it.

For a moment, they just stood there, breathing hard, the way people do when they've outrun something they can't see.

Then Kate grabbed her.

She pulled Ariel into her arms so hard the girl gave a soft "oof," then clung back just as tightly. For a few seconds, neither of them spoke. Kate buried her face in her daughter's hair, breathing in soap and fear and cold sweat.

"Are you okay?" Kate managed finally, pulling back enough to check her face, her hands, her arms. "Did you see him?"

Ariel shook her head, curls bouncing. Her eyes were huge and dark. "No. I didn't see anybody. I heard the bells a couple of times, and a can... I thought it was the wind. I stayed behind the fridge just like you said. I swear, Mom, I didn't open the door for anyone."

"I know," Kate said immediately. "You did perfectly. You did exactly what you were supposed to do."

She tried to keep her voice level, but it came out rough, frayed around the edges.

Ariel's gaze searched her face. "You saw something out there, didn't you?"

Kate hesitated. She thought of the rocking chair turned toward the glass, the bootprints, the smoldering cigarette, the bell laid out like a little shrine.

She wanted to lie, to make Ariel feel safe.

But she couldn't.

"He was on the porch," Kate said quietly. "Sat in the rocking chair. Smoked a few cigarettes. Took one of our bells and left it out there for me to find." She swallowed. "He was watching through the front window while I was gone."

Ariel's shoulders crept up toward her ears. "But...the curtains were closed. And I stayed behind the fridge!"

"Curtains don't matter if he can see your shadow moving," Kate replied. "Listen to me—" She caught Ariel's face gently in both hands. "You did everything right. This is on me, not you. I shouldn't have gone off alone."

Something in Ariel's expression loosened. "Did you...were you able to track him?"

Kate shook her head. "I found signs, but he's playing games. Circling. Leaving little...breadcrumbs." She huffed out a humorless laugh. "Hansel and Gretel with a nicotine addiction."

Ariel glanced toward the front window, as if she could see the purple rocking chair through the wall. "Is he still out there close?"

"I don't know," Kate replied honestly. "The cigarette was still warm, but the prints were already starting to dry at the edges. He was here...then he left. He wanted me to know I missed him by a hair."

Ariel wrapped her arms around her middle. "He could have—" She stopped, throat working.

"I know." The words tasted like metal. "He could have. But he didn't."

They stood beside the barricaded door while the cabin ticked around them—the soft pop from the stove, a faint creak from the rafters above.

Finally, Kate moved to the window beside the door. She stayed to one side, flattening herself against the wall, and eased the curtain back with two fingers just enough to see the corner of the porch.

The rocking chair rocked slightly in the breeze, empty now. The bell and cigarette butts still sat on the railing like a tiny, evil still life.

She let the curtain fall.

"Okay," she said, turning back. "Here's what we're going to do. No more running off alone. No more playing hunter."

"Then what?" Ariel whispered.

"We rest," Kate said. "We eat. We keep the fire low and the doors locked, and we stay away from the windows. He likes to play games." Her jaw tightened. "If he comes back, it'll be because he thinks we're scared and tired."

"Aren't we?" Ariel asked.

Kate gave a short laugh that was almost a sob. "Oh, absolutely. But he doesn't get to see that part."

She nodded toward the kitchen. "Show me your setup."

Ariel led her around the table to the corner behind the refrigerator. The little nest made Kate's throat go tight: the pillow, the afghan, the battered copy of The Secret Garden lying open and face-down, its spine cracked from years of reading.

"A bulletproof pillow fort," Ariel said weakly, attempting a smile.

"It's perfect," Kate said, meaning it. "You picked the best cover in the house."

She crouched there for a second, seeing the kitchen from Ariel's height—the slice of the front door visible through the gap, the angle that gave a partial view of the living room without exposing her body.

She did everything right, Kate thought again. Every single thing. And he still—still—almost had her.

The thought made something hot flare up behind her eyes. Rage, this time, not fear.

She stood and ruffled Ariel's hair. "Go sit on the couch where I can see you. I'm going to heat up some soup, and then we'll talk about our next move."

Ariel hesitated. "Is there one...a next move?"

"Oh, there's a next move, all right," Kate said with a confidence she didn't feel. "He wants to rattle us. Make us feel helpless." She glanced toward the front porch where the ghost of his bootprints lingered in her mind. "We're going to let him believe he succeeded. For a little while."

"And then?" Ariel asked.

"And then," Kate said, reaching for a pot, "we're going to make very sure he regrets not finishing what he started today."

She popped open a jar of homemade chili. Soon, the air was redolent with the scent of beef and spices. Outside, the bells on the lines gave small, nervous jingles in the wind. Things seemed almost normal, if you didn't know what had just happened to that rocking chair.

Kate got the crackers from the kitchen pantry and put them on the table to have with the chili. She got out two colorful bowls and a funny little silver sugar spoon that Ariel insisted was her "chili spoon."

Ariel pulled out a sleeve of saltines and opened them, only to pull too hard and have them fly all over the table. Her eyes filled with tears that Kate pretended not to see.

"You don't know your own strength," she teased lightly. "Have you been secretly lifting weights in the middle of the night?"

Ariel sniffed and forced a crooked smile. "Midnight powerlifting. Very exclusive program."

For a little while, they would pretend that everything was okay.

Chapter 30

The chili was warm and spicy, exactly as it should be.

The cabin was barricaded like a frontier fort, and it shouldn't have been.

So they ignored it.

For the first time in days, the silence didn't feel razor-sharp.

They cleared the dishes from the table and put the remainder of the chili in the fridge. Kate washed, and Ariel dried with a brightly colored dish towel.

"All right," Kate said, forcing brightness into her voice. "Cards or dominoes?"

Ariel blinked at her over a cracker. "Dominoes. I'm terrible at cards, and you hustle me every time."

Kate snorted. "You cannot hustle your own child, sweetheart."

"You absolutely can," Ariel said, dragging the little wooden box out of the cabinet by the fridge. "You hustle me at Uno every time we play."

Kate cleared a patch of table between the two Glocks, nudging them aside as if they were just another pair of salt shakers. She pushed the guns just far enough away to keep them out of immediate view so they could act as though they were playing a game and that they didn't each have a pistol within arm's reach.

Ariel set the dominoes on the table with a flourish. "Let's pretend," she said, sitting across from her mother and trying to smile, "that we aren't literally barricaded in our house like it's the zombie apocalypse."

Kate matched her smile. "Easy. Watch this." She pointed to the armoire blocking the door. "That's just a rustic decorative piece."

"And the dining chairs stacked in front of the back door?"

"Obviously modern art."

"And the fishing-line tripwire across the clearing?"

"That's..." Kate paused, then shrugged. "Seasonal décor."

Ariel laughed—a real one this time. Thin, tired, but real. She continued turning all the dominoes face down so they could draw.

Kate leaned back in her chair and stretched her legs out, trying to let her shoulders drop. The normalcy felt absurd. Almost indulgent.

She glanced at her daughter over the line of dominoes. There was finally a bit of color in Ariel's cheeks.

"We're preppers," Kate said lightly, setting down her first piece. "We can outlast the zombies for a long time."

Ariel parted her lips to respond, then shut them again, eyes flicking toward the window. The curtain was drawn. They both pretended it made a difference.

"Yeah," Ariel said eventually, lining up her tile with deliberate care. "We're like... Olympic-level at waiting out crazy zombies in the woods."

Kate laughed. "Exactly. This is practically our hobby."

A gust hit the side of the cabin, making one of the tripwire bells jingle faintly.

Both of them went still.

Just for a second.

Then Ariel carefully placed another domino. "Wind," she said quietly.

Kate nodded, teeth clenched. "Wind."

They played three rounds. Ariel lost two, won one, and crowed triumphantly at her victory. Kate let herself bask in the sound—the unsteady laugh of a child pretending to be brave.

Kate got up to make popcorn on the stovetop.

Behind her, Ariel sprawled on the couch, wrapped burrito-style in her afghan, pretending not to watch the shadows under the front door.

The corn popped faster and faster until it was done. Kate tossed in real butter and put it back on the stove to let it melt. She grabbed two diet root beers from the fridge.

For a few minutes, everything felt almost normal.

Almost peaceful. Almost safe.

Kate wiped her hands, leaned her hip against the counter, and allowed herself one quiet thought:

Maybe we can get through the night without anything else happening.

Outside, the wind brushed weakly against the eaves.

The bells stayed still.

For now.

...

They watched a silly old sitcom on Kate's laptop with the volume so low it was mostly just a murmur. They weren't really watching it. They were listening—harder than they ever had in their lives.

Every groan of the timbers.

Every whisper of wind.

Every tinkle of the bells.

Ariel tried to laugh at a joke on the screen, but the sound came out thin and cracked.

Kate pulled the curtains tighter, making sure no light leaked out. Then she made another perimeter check inside the cabin—windows latched, doors secured, armoire braced against the front door, and kitchen chairs stacked against the back door.

Her shadow flickered across the walls, long and thin in the lamplight.

Ariel curled sideways on the couch, blanket around her shoulders, popcorn bowl in her lap. "Are we gonna sleep at all tonight?" she wondered.

"We can take shifts," Kate answered softly, knowing she wasn't going to wake Ariel in the middle of the night to sit there in terror while she slept.

Ariel nodded, but her eyes didn't leave the front door.

The hours crept by.

The wind calmed.

The trees settled.

The bells outside gave only the occasional soft, innocent jingle—nothing sharp, nothing deliberate.

Kate forced herself to rest for one hour, lying on her side on the couch with her boots still on, the Glock under her hand. She didn't truly sleep—she hovered in that floaty, brittle place where your mind is still listening even as your breathing slows.

Ariel watched the windows, fighting yawns. At some point, she crawled from the couch to the floor behind the refrigerator and dozed sitting upright, blanket wrapped around her shoulders like a cape.

It was a terrible, aching kind of night, but, as all nights do, it passed.

Eventually, the darkness softened.

The cabin's edges reappeared.

A faint, pale glow crept through the cracks of the curtains.

Ariel stirred first, rubbing her face. "Is it morning?"

Kate sat up instantly, blinking hard. "Looks like it."

She checked the door. Still locked. The armoire was undisturbed. She peeked through the curtain. Nothing new on the porch.

For now, the world looked ordinary.

Kate exhaled a long, shuddering breath.

They had made it through the night.

But morning would bring new dangers.

She felt it in her very bones.

Chapter 31

Morning light seeped through the curtains in thin, watery bands. It made the cabin look gentler than it had any right to, given the current situation. Kate stood at the kitchen window, not in front of it, but angled sideways, careful of her silhouette. She watched the fog rise off the yard. For her coffee, she had chosen a purple mug that said, *I came. I saw. I forgot what I was doing* in a script that looked handwritten.

"It looks so... normal," Ariel said quietly, coming up beside her with her blanket still around her shoulders.

Kate nodded, though her chest stayed tight. "Normal's a tricky thing. It fools you."

Ariel yawned and shuffled to the stove. "Can I please have coffee, too?"

Kate hesitated. Normally, she didn't let Ariel drink a full cup of coffee—just a sip here and there of her mother's. She was inclined to say yes today, but her thoughts scattered because of where Ariel stood while making the request. She was right in front of the window, where her silhouette might be clear to someone outside.

The idea of her daughter standing near a window—even for a second, much less directly in front of one—made Kate's skin crawl.

But normalcy mattered. Small rituals mattered. They steadied the hands.

"Yeah," Kate said softly. "That sounds nice. You can join me for a cup."

Ariel busied herself pouring coffee from the pot into a mug, adding cream, then sugar, doing everything carefully, almost ceremonially, as if making coffee could anchor the world in place.

Kate did another sweep of the cabin exterior, peeking through the windows.

The tripwire bells looked untouched.

The teal rocking chair sat still in its corner, now in the proper position overlooking the forest as Kate had placed it the day before.

No fresh footprints were obvious.

No shadows moved between the trees.

"So... what now?" Ariel asked tentatively over the rim of her yellow mug. "We can't just stay here like this forever."

Kate leaned her palms on the counter. "We'll figure something out. But for now, we breathe. And we stay alert."

Ariel poured two mugs and slid one across the counter toward her mother. She tried for a smile, saying hopefully, "Maybe he really did leave."

Kate didn't answer. She didn't want to destroy that small bit of optimism, but she also didn't want to lie.

Instead, she lifted the curtain one more inch and scanned the driveway, as she had a dozen times already.

Empty.

"He's gone," Ariel said again, more hopeful now.

Kate took a slow sip of coffee.

Maybe, she thought, without conviction.

"Maybe," she said aloud, in a tone more cheerful than she felt.

A deep quiet had settled over the mountain, too quiet, almost painted-on quiet.

A quiet that made Kate's instincts twitch.

Then she heard it.

The crunch of tires on gravel. Slow. Heavy. Unfamiliar.

Ariel straightened so fast her mug clinked against the counter.

Kate's stomach dropped.

They weren't expecting anyone.

No one knew they were here.

She grabbed her firearm, and Ariel followed suit.

Kate moved to the living room window, expecting to see Logan's truck pulling in just to mock them.

She was stunned when, instead, a sheriff's SUV rolled into view, half-fogged headlights cutting through the trees.

Ariel whispered, "Mom... is that for real?"

Kate's voice was barely audible. "I don't know yet."

She hardly dared to hope.

The SUV rolled to a slow stop at the top of the driveway, tires cracking over frost-stiff gravel. A door creaked open.

Kate and Ariel both ducked low.

A silhouette moved past the headlights—broad shoulders, uniform jacket, hat. He paused to look up at the cabin, hands planted on his duty belt, stance casual. Too casual for Kate's liking. He didn't seem urgent or alarmed.

That bothered her.

He should have shown more tension if he knew a crime was being committed, especially if Mr. Slocum's body had been discovered.

"Mom...?" Ariel whispered again.

Kate's heartbeat thudded in her ears. She tried to sort through her instincts—years of them, sharpened by experience and regret and survival.

Something about this felt off.

Not wrong.

Just... misaligned.

Kate watched from beside the window as the sheriff (*Was he really the sheriff? Was she crazy for wondering that?* she pondered) started up the path toward the porch, boots crunching softly. He moved at an easy pace, as though approaching a home where nothing bad ever happened, where no one was hunted through the forest by a man with a knife and a grudge.

Kate motioned for Ariel to get behind the fridge.

Ariel nodded once and slipped silently into her hiding place.

Kate stayed angled away from the window as the knock came—firm, polite, measured.

Not frantic. Not desperate.

Just... neighborly.

A pause.

Then a voice, muffled through the door. "Sheriff's Department. Anyone home?"

Kate pressed her back against the wall near the door, gun held low but ready. Her pulse hammered. Was she being paranoid?

Yes, she told herself unconvincingly.

Still, something prickled at the base of her skull—the same sensation she'd felt in the woods when she realized Logan was circling her trail rather than running from her.

"Should we answer?" Ariel whispered.

"No," Kate mouthed. "Not yet."

The sheriff knocked again, a little louder but still without urgency. "Anybody home? I've been trying to reach the occupants here. We've been asked to make a notification. I'm here to make sure you're all right."

Kate's gut twisted.

Her voice nearly cracked with relief.

Maybe. Maybe this was finally help.

She took a slow breath to steady herself and called through the door, "Identify yourself, please."

The sheriff stepped back a bit, posture shifting as though to give her space. "Deputy Collins, ma'am. Henderson County Sheriff's Office." His tone was calm, practiced. "I'd be obliged if you opened the door. Just need to make sure you're safe."

Kate hesitated only a second longer.

He used the word obliged.

Old-fashioned. Polite. The kind of thing a real mountain deputy might say.

She flicked her gaze toward the front window, catching a glimpse of the vehicle again. It boasted real plates, real markings, and an intact light bar. Not a trap. Not Logan's beat-up truck.

Her shoulders relaxed, and she pulled the curtain aside. "It'll just take me a minute," she called, then began to push the big armoire out of the way.

She unlatched the top lock.

Ariel's breath hitched audibly behind her.

Kate reached for the bottom lock, feeling something in her chest unclench for the first time in days.

Hope.

She opened the door just enough to see the deputy—and let him see her.

And that's when she saw it.

Beyond the deputy's shoulder, a figure stepped into view from behind the SUV.

Tall.

Lean.

Familiar as a recurring bad dream.

Logan.

Her face froze into something that had once been a smile.

He lifted two fingers to his forehead in a mocking little salute.

Kate swallowed a gasp and stepped back a fraction, the breath punched out of her.

He wasn't rushing the porch.

He wasn't charging the door.

He was waiting.

Waiting for her to open it.

Because the sheriff wasn't in danger yet.

But he would be.

Kate's voice cracked as she screamed, "Behind you!"

Chapter 32

The deputy's brows knit at her tone.

"Ma'am?"

"Behind you!" Kate shouted again, louder now, sharp with panic.

To his credit, Deputy Collins reacted fast. His hand snapped to the grip of his holstered weapon as he half-turned, instinct dragging his gaze toward the driveway.

But instinct wasn't enough.

Logan was already moving.

He came up the porch steps with a speed that felt wrong—too fast, too quiet. A blur of motion, something wolfish in the way he closed the distance. The deputy's eyes widened as understanding finally landed.

"Hey—HE—"

The word strangled off as Logan slammed into him.

They hit the top step hard.

The deputy's gun never cleared the holster.

Logan's knife did.

Kate saw the flash of metal—just a glint in the fog—before Logan drove the blade up under the deputy's ribcage. A wet, sucking sound followed. The deputy's breath hitched as if the air had been punched from him. His knees buckled, but Logan caught him, holding him upright.

Using him.

A shield.

Ariel screamed and ducked back behind the refrigerator.

Kate froze for half a heartbeat—shock, terror—then remembered the weight in her hands. She raised the pistol with both arms locked and aimed straight at Logan's head.

"Let him GO!" she screamed.

Logan looked at her, eyes bright blue with something manic, and winked.

He withdrew the knife slowly.

Then slashed it across the deputy's torso again.

A horrible, hollow sound tore out of the man—half breath, half disbelief—before his body sagged forward. Logan eased him down one step, almost gently.

Then he lifted his eyes to Kate.

The smile he gave her was slow. Wrong. Tender in the way a predator is tender with something it already considers dead.

"Morning, family," he said, grinning widely, voice soft as smoke.

Kate raised the Glock, rage humming through her hard enough to blur her vision—

—but Logan shifted, pulling the deputy's collapsing body between them. The man groaned weakly, blood bubbling at his lips.

"Go ahead, Katie," Logan said lightly. "Shoot me."

Kate's breath caught.

He was right. She couldn't risk it—not while the deputy was still alive, not while there was even a chance she could save him.

"Do it!" Logan bellowed. "Shoot me!"

He backed down a step, dragging the wounded man with him, grinning as Kate tried—and failed—to find a clean angle.

"See?" he coaxed. "You still care what happens to people. That's your problem. Always has been."

Kate lunged for the door—

—but Logan flung the deputy's body sideways, letting it crash into the porch railing with a sickening thud.

Then he charged.

Kate barely slammed the door in time, throwing her weight against it as the first impact rattled the hinges.

"Ariel!" she shouted. "Help me! NOW!"

Ariel was already moving, shoving the armoire with her shoulder, tears streaking her face. The furniture scraped across the floor, inch by inch, while Kate held the door with everything she had.

Another slam. Harder.

"You're mine, Kate!" Logan sang. "Don't make this harder!"

Kate braced her boots, shoved back, the door shuddering under the assault. The smell of blood—sharp and metallic—leaked through the cracks.

"He killed him—he killed the cop—" Ariel sobbed.

"I know!" Kate shouted. "We can't think about that. PUSH!"

Logan hit the door again. And again. Each blow tighter, more focused. Testing. Learning.

Kate felt her shoulder start to give. Her feet slipped.

And in that razor-thin moment, she knew—

This wasn't about hiding. Or waiting. Or hoping.

This was the endgame.

She leaned her hip into the door and shoved the armoire fully into place. The barricade wasn't perfect—but it would hold. For now.

He is not walking in through my front door.

Outside, Logan returned to the deputy.

Kate watched through the window as he kicked the wounded man onto his back, tore the radio from his belt, and crushed it under his heel—making sure she saw.

Then he sauntered over to the cruiser, puncturing two of its tires.

He came back to the deputy and stripped him of all his weapons. The gun. The taser. The nightstick.

Mockery, one piece at a time.

Then Logan bent down to rifle through the deputy's pockets.

And missed the twitch.

Just once.

Pain cut through the haze enough to wake Collins fully. As Logan leaned closer, the deputy acted.

With a broken, desperate cry, he drove his folding knife upward, burying it deep into Logan's upper thigh—high and brutal.

For a split second, Logan didn't register it.

Then he did.

A raw, animal sound ripped from his throat. His leg buckled. Blood spilled fast and hot. He staggered back, clutching his thigh, the knife still jutting obscenely from the wound.

Kate gasped. Ariel whimpered.

Logan yanked the blade free and stumbled toward the treeline, fury twisting his face.

Not an artery, unfortunately, Kate thought grimly.

But bad.

Bad enough.

Logan vanished into the fog-choked woods, limping and cursing, a wounded thing retreating to cover, his smeared footprints dripping dark and steady into the trees.

Kate didn't watch him go.

Her instincts screamed "NOW!"

She turned to Ariel and ordered briskly, "Cover me. Don't fire unless you see him. But if you do—don't hesitate."

Ariel nodded, jaw trembling but eyes locked in.

Kate shoved the armoire aside and bolted down the steps, boots skidding in blood.

Deputy Collins lay crumpled at the bottom, breathing in wet, broken pulls. Pink foam bubbled at his mouth.

"Stay with me," Kate said, sliding an arm behind his shoulders.

"No... go back inside..." he rasped.

"No way," she said. "You're not dying on my porch."

She hauled him up, bracing her body under his weight, muscles burning, breath tearing out of her chest.

"I'll try," he gasped.

"Good man."

Step by step. Drag. Lift. Haul.

"Get your feet under you, Deputy!"

He tried manfully and got up another step with her pulling.

He began to sag in her arm.

She hollered, "MOVE YOUR ASS, DEPUTY!"

It worked. It sparked the last bit of impetus he needed to get up the final step.

With Ariel rushing to help, they dragged him across the threshold and into the cabin.

Alive.

Chapter 33

Logan staggered through the trees, breath hissing between clenched teeth.

His world narrowed to pain. It was white-hot, pulsing, radiating down his leg with every limping step.

Stupid. Careless.

He hadn't expected the deputy to still be alive, let alone to have the strength to drive a blade into the tender area of Logan's inner thigh.

That kind of cut bled like a bastard.

Logan pressed both hands over the wound, fingers slipping in the warmth, and snarled low in his throat. His vision shimmered at the edges, a red haze he forced himself to blink through.

Pain was manageable. Pain was temporary. Pain was a thing weak men feared.

He wasn't weak.

Not anymore.

He moved deeper into the woods, away from the cabin, away from Kate's silhouette in the window. He could still feel her eyes on him. Could almost imagine her breath catching when she saw him hurt. She cared. He knew she did. That's why she hadn't shot him. That's why she'd screamed. That's why she looked at him with all that trembling emotion she tried to pretend was hatred.

She wasn't ready yet.

He found a fallen log and collapsed onto it, forcing his hands to steady. The knife wound wasn't the worst he'd ever had. Prison had offered plenty of opportunities to learn what the body could tolerate.

But the deputy had gotten him really high up on his leg—too high. Right near the groin. The muscle contracted every time he breathed. Thankfully, it had missed his femoral artery.

He was lucky.

No.

Not luck.

Destiny.

He knew the way he'd dodged death was a sign that reuniting with his family was meant to be. If it wasn't, he'd be bleeding out in Kate's front yard right now.

Logan sucked air through his teeth and reached into his pocket for his small kit. Prison habit. Always carry something. A scrap of cloth. A strip of tape. A length of ripped bedsheet.

He tore the fabric with his teeth and wrapped it tight around his thigh, knotting it until the bleeding slowed. The pain flared so hard he nearly threw up.

The forest swayed a little. He closed his eyes. He couldn't stop it. He leaned over the back of the log and emptied his stomach, leaving his mouth feeling soiled and sour. He spat, tasting bile and copper.

Good.

An empty stomach meant fewer distractions.

Kate would try to help that deputy. She'd waste min- utes—maybe more—patching him up. She'd check his breathing, his heart rate, his wounds. She'd try to save him.

Logan smiled. His woman was so kind.

Good.

The more time she spent on the dying man, the more time Logan had to prepare.

To circle back.

To correct the mistake.

He thought of Ariel—her scream, the way she hid behind the refrigerator like a frightened rabbit.

Their daughter.

He hated that she had become afraid of him. But she would come around.

Children always came around in the end

He leaned back on the log, breathing shallowly. The fog drifted through the pines, cool against his burning skin.

He didn't mind the wound.

Pain sharpened the world.

Made him focused.

And now that he'd felt Kate's fear again—seen it in her eyes—he'd never stop. Not until she came home.

Not until they were all together, the way it was sup- posed to be.

He forgave her for sending him to prison. It had been a terrible misunderstanding. He had thought of her every single day of his sentence and had pictures of Kate and Ariel taped to his wall.

"My family," he'd say to the other inmates when they noticed the pictures. "I don't want my daughter to see me like this," he'd rationalize when they asked him why they never visited.

Logan pushed himself upright, ignoring the agony screaming through his leg. The bandage was already warm and wet again. He didn't have much time.

He wiped his bloody hands on the dead leaves, tightened the makeshift bandage one more notch, and grabbed a water bottle from the backpack he'd stocked with supplies stolen from Kate's cabin over the past week. He was losing blood, and he knew he needed to replenish his fluids.

When the time was right, he'd start limping back toward the cabin.

He wasn't done.

Not even close.

First, he was going to lie down and think of Kate's face—set, trembling, trying so hard to be firm while she played hard to get.

Chapter 34

With one last surge, Kate muscled Collins over the threshold. They went down together, hard, hitting the cabin floor with a thud that rattled the picture frames. For a moment, she lay on the floor with his torso across her legs, trying to suck air into her own burning lungs.

Ariel slammed the door shut, and that spurred Kate into action. She wiggled out from under the deputy.

She and Ariel replaced the armoire where it secured the door.

Then Kate was all business.

"The kit we need is in the basement," Kate told her. "This time I'm going to cover you."

They shoved the heavy kitchen table away from the basement door and removed the Molly bar. Kate flipped on the light and went down first, checking all the shadowy corners.

"All clear," she called out.

Ariel sprinted toward the shelves.

"Red dufflel!" Kate ordered.

Ariel grabbed it and ran up the stairs, Kate close behind, walking backward, gun fixed forward just in case trouble showed up. She didn't think he'd be able to squeeze in, but he might be able to get off a few shots through the broken window.

She breathed a sigh of relief when they were able to barricade the basement door again.

All business, Kate scrubbed her hands at the sink, fast but thorough—the prepper instinct drilled into her bones. Blood and dirt spiraled down the drain.

"I'm going to need your help, Ari," she told the girl, who nodded brusquely. "Unzip the bag and go get all the clean towels."

Ariel raced away, and Kate could hear her open the linen closet in the bathroom. She soon returned with an armload of linens.

"Now go get some water boiling, honey." Kate didn't need the water but it would give Ariel a sense of purpose.

His breaths were fast, shallow, bubbling. The wound under his ribs made a faint sucking sound with every inhale—the unmistakable sign that air was entering the chest cavity. She cut open his uniform shirt with trauma shears she pulled from the bag.

"Collapsed lung," she talked herself through it, remembering the course she'd taken on advanced trauma care. "Open pneumothorax. I need to seal it."

Ariel returned with the kettle and a large bowl.

"Look for a light brown envelope that says CHEST SEAL in big black letters."

Kate told Collins, "Hey, my friend, I know that was horrible, me dragging you up those stairs. I'm going to do everything I can to help you. Unfortunately, it's also going to suck."

He smiled through the pain and said through gritted teeth, "I have a little girl and a wife to get back to."

"I'll do my best."

Ariel located the chest seal and held onto it while Kate blotted the wound. Blood foamed at the edges with every inhale. She soaked the corner of another towel in the clean water and patted around the wound to clear away blood. She dried the area thoroughly so the seal would stick.

"Ariel, grab the flashlight. High angle. I need to see."

Ariel clicked it on with shaking hands.

Kate tore open the package containing the chest seal with her teeth, peeled the backing off, and rapidly adhered the plastic over the wound, smoothing the edges with her palms to create an airtight seal.

The bubbling sound stopped.

Collins gasped—one long, shocked inhale—then continued breathing shallowly.

Kate cheered him on. "You're okay. That lung will reinflate some on its own now."

Next wound, she thought.

A gash in his lower left abdomen was still seeping blood and needed to be packed.

"This one's going to hurt like hell," she warned.

"Your bedside manner is terrible," the deputy joked weakly.

Collins groaned as she packed the wound with sterile gauze, strip by strip. Once filled, she placed a pressure dressing over it and secured it with an elastic wrap.

She checked his pulse. Thready. Fast. Cold sweat beaded his forehead.

Shock.

She elevated his legs with blankets and slid a pillow under his head.

"Stay awake, Collins," she ordered. "What's your first name?"

"Evan," he whispered, barely audible.

"Good," she said, smoothing his hair back. "Stay with me, Evan. You did good out there. Damn good."

Ariel hovered behind her, voice trembling. "Is... is he going to die?"

Kate looked at her daughter—steady gaze, calm tone, no lies.

"Not if I have anything to say about it."

Then she leaned close to Ariel and whispered, "I'm going to call for help on the deputy's SUV radio. Logan didn't break the one in the truck."

Ariel's eyes widened. "Mom... are you sure?"

Kate nodded. "We're calling for help. Evan needs better care than I can give him. I want you to cover me the best you can from the porch, okay?"

Ariel nodded.

Once again, they shoved the heavy armoire away from the door, this time leaving only enough room for Kate to squeeze through sideways.

"If Logan shows up when I'm in the cop car, I'm going to lock the doors and stay out there. You get back inside and lock up."

"But, Mom—"

Kate interrupted her with just a look.

She emerged onto the porch and scanned the area.

Logan was somewhere in that fog.

Bleeding.

Angry.

And coming back.

But she couldn't see him, so once Ariel gave the all-clear from the porch, Kate raced to the police car.

The door was unlocked. She got in and locked the doors behind her. She snatched up the handset.

"Hello? HELLO? Can anybody hear me?"

All she heard from the radio was crackling. She looked closer at the handset and discovered a button labeled TALK. She pressed it and called out again.

The radio crackled.

Nobody.

Tears filled her eyes.

She was so very tired.

Then the radio flared to life. "This is an official channel. Identify yourself."

Kate laughed with relief. She used the last of her emotional reserves to give her name and address.

"Your officer is hurt—Deputy Collins. I'm doing my best to help him, but you need to come fast. You need an ambulance."

"Hold on this line," ordered the voice from the radio.

"I can't," Kate replied, not at all intimidated. "It's not safe here. Please come quickly. I have to go back inside with your deputy."

She put the handset back in its cradle, opened the door, and looked around. Ariel nodded from the porch and gave her the all-clear.

Kate headed for the porch at a quick trot, too tired to move faster.

A stick cracked in the forest, loud as a gunshot.

She found her energy then and ran for the porch like a host of demons was behind her.

Chapter 35

Kate slammed the door behind her. The frame shuddered. She fell against it, chest heaving. It felt like the very fog was clinging to her clothes, cold and damp. The metallic taste of fear was still sharp on her tongue.

Ariel lowered the pistol, shoulders shaking. "Mom?"

Kate nodded once, holding up one finger to say wordlessly, just a minute. She was unable to speak for a moment as she sucked air into her lungs. She locked the door, slid the deadbolt home, then replaced the armoire with Ariel's help.

Only when the barricade was in place did she feel like she could speak.

"I reached someone," she said finally. "Help is coming."

Collins and Ariel both sagged with relief. Collins shut his eyes.

Then Ariel's expression darkened. "But Logan—"

"He's still out there." Kate's voice held no tremor, just truth. "And he's coming back."

A faint, distant scrape sounded outside—something against the siding. Not a full attack.

Just a reminder.

Kate closed her eyes and forced herself not to flinch.

She knelt beside Collins. He was pale, breathing shallow, but alive.

"Evan," she said softly, touching his shoulder.

His eyelids fluttered. "Still here... ma'am." His eyes unfocused for a second, then snapped back.

"You did good. I'm going to move you someplace safer."

His brow furrowed. "Safer than the floor?"

"Yeah," Kate whispered, and despite everything, her voice warmed. "Come on. Let's get you tucked away. I'm depending on you, Evan. I need you breathing steady, and I need you keeping my daughter safe. I'm going to prop you up so you can breathe better, and you are going to protect Ariel. Got it?"

"Yes, ma'am," Collins made an effort to salute, then grimaced in pain.

She motioned to Ariel, and together they eased Collins upright. He groaned, clutching his abdomen, but didn't protest. Kate took most of his weight, guiding him toward the refrigerator.

Ariel pulled blankets aside to clear space behind it—her old hiding spot. The place she'd run earlier today when Logan attacked the deputy.

They settled Collins down gently. He slumped against the wall, breathing unevenly.

Kate crouched and checked his chest seal—edges adhered, no leak. She touched the abdominal bandage—still holding. His skin was cool but not clammy.

Shock, but controlled.

"You're holding steady," she murmured. "Just stay awake for me."

He swallowed. "Trying."

Kate reached into the first aid kit and pulled out a small foil packet of glucose gel. She squeezed a bit onto her glove and touched it to his lips.

"Just a little," she coached. "It'll help."

He nodded shakily and let her feed him a few drops.

Ariel watched, clutching her pistol in both hands, pointing it safely toward the floor. "Is there anything else we can do for him?"

Kate brushed a thumb along Ariel's cheek. "You're doing everything right. You're helping. That matters. Can you please keep him talking? Ask him about his little girl."

Ariel blinked fast, then nodded.

Outside, something thudded lightly on the porch. She distinctly heard a step, then another sound, like a boot dragging.

His injured leg, Kate thought.

The boards gave a faint answering creak, as if the porch itself recognized him.

Logan was testing their perimeter again.

Kate felt rage bubble up. How dare he be on her porch? Her jaw stiffened stubbornly.

Time was running out.

She grabbed three boxes of ammo and some extra magazines she had in the same drawer, then sat on the floor beside Ariel and Evan.

"Are we... are we getting ready?" Ariel whispered.

Kate didn't answer with words. She opened a box and began loading magazines with quick, practiced movements. The soft click of each round sliding home echoed through the cabin like a heartbeat.

Ariel helped, her hands trembling as she fed bullets into a spare mag using a speed-loading device. One round slipped from her fingers, but she steadied herself and loaded the next cleanly.

Evan held out a shaking hand for a magazine and a box of ammo. Kate gave him those, along with a speed loader.

Kate handed Ariel a full magazine.

"Pocket it," she said gently. "Just in case."

Ariel obeyed.

Kate secured two mags at her belt, checked the Glock's chamber, then laid the machete on the table. She wiped its blade with a towel, calming herself with the familiar, methodical motion.

Collins rasped from behind the fridge, "Ma'am... Kate..."

She returned to him, crouching again.

His eyes were clearer now—pain-bright but focused.

"If he comes through that door," Collins said hoarsely, "I can still... shoot. Don't leave me useless."

Kate hesitated, but only for a single heartbeat.

"Ariel, how would you feel about getting your chance to tase Logan?"

Ariel looked mutinous for a flash, then handed Collins the gun, butt first. She pressed it into his trembling hand.

Kate said earnestly, "I'm going to get you back to your little girl. I need you to keep mine safe."

His jaw tightened. "I can do that."

Their eyes locked, two parents, determined to get out of this situation alive.

Ariel knelt beside him, taking her position: tucked, hidden, heart pounding, but brave.

Kate brushed Ariel's hair back and kissed her forehead.

"You watch him," Kate ordered gently. "You stay hidden. No matter what you hear. No matter what happens."

Ariel's eyes filled with tears. "Mom, don't go."

Kate cupped her face in both hands. "I have to. If I stay here, he'll force his way in. He'll be in here with you. If I go out there... I choose where the fight happens. I choose the battlefield."

Ariel swallowed hard, nodding. "Please come back."

Kate smiled, fierce and soft. "That's the plan."

She stood, holstered her Glock, clipped the flashlight to her pocket, and checked the front window.

The fog was a wall.

Silent.

Waiting.

It was as if the cabin itself was holding its breath.

"Kate..." Collins called weakly. "...End it. It's you or him."

She looked back at him, at Ariel pressed against his side.

"I will."

Kate made a gap she could squeeze through. She placed her hand on the doorknob.

Drew a breath.

Then...

CRACK.

The unmistakable sound of breaking glass came from somewhere on the other side of the cabin.

Chapter 36

The sound came like a sharp crack—one distinct shatter in the quiet of their anticipation.

Kate spun toward the hallway, Glock already half-raised.

Glass.

Not close.

Not the kitchen.

Ariel's room.

Her first thought was immediate and feral:

He's inside.

Ariel gasped behind her. Collins sucked a wet breath through his teeth.

"Ariel, you stay and take care of Evan." Kate didn't look behind her to see if Ariel had obeyed.

She moved toward the hall instinctively—two steps—muscles coiled, breath tight—and then she froze.

Because something else followed the silence.

A soft hiss.

A faint pop.

An unfamiliar crackling sound.

She tilted her head, trying to make out what Logan was doing.

Then she saw it: a curl of gray drifting out from the bottom of the closed bedroom door. It came and went, cautiously, insidiously, like the tongue of a serpent testing the air outside the bedroom.

It took several seconds—too many—for her brain to compute what her eyes already knew.

Kate stared at the thin smoky ribbon rolling across the floorboards, slow as spilled ink spreading on paper.

No footsteps.

No breathing.

No creaking floorboards from an intruder.

Just... smoke.

Growing thicker by the second. Making her throat ache. Causing her face to feel hot, almost blistered.

Her heart plummeted.

"No," she breathed, half anguished cry, half prayer. "Oh, God—no."

A louder crack came from inside the bedroom. A whoosh. A bright lick of orange light snapped under the doorframe like some hellish animal trying to escape—feral, hungry.

That lunatic had actually set her cabin on fire.

Ariel's voice wavered from behind her, in the doorway of the kitchen, small and breaking. "Mom... that's my room. What—"

Kate didn't let her finish.

She whipped around and grabbed Ariel's shoulder, shoving her gently but urgently back toward the kitchen. "Get back. Stay with Evan. Keep the door covered. Do not move."

The bedroom door rattled once—then audibly warped, the wood heating and bending as flames crawled along its far side.

Heat spread through the hallway like a rising exhale.

Their sanctuary—their haven—the place that had sheltered them after their lives blew up—was burning from the inside out.

Smoke thickened by the second, rolling through the hallway in dirty gray waves. The acrid bite clawed at Kate's throat; she swallowed hard and kept moving. The bedroom door groaned, bowing outward as heat chewed at its hinges.

He wasn't coming in. He was forcing them to come out.

Kate didn't waste another heartbeat.

She ran back to Collins and Ariel. "We have to get out. Now."

Ariel's eyes were wide, watery, but sharp. "Tell me what to do."

"Back door," Kate said.

Quickly, Ariel shoved the vintage Hoosier cabinet out of its place as a barricade.

"Good. On my count." Kate squatted down level with the deputy. He was stubbornly remaining conscious despite the brutal pain he must be in. "We have to get out of here and it's going to suck," she told him kindly.

Collins replied roughly, "No, you two should leave me here and run up into the woods." He glanced compellingly at Ariel.

"Do you think I dragged your heavy butt up those stairs and did my best doctoring to date so I could leave you here?" Kate demanded. Her voice brooked no disobedience when she bellowed, "Get up, Deputy!"

He nodded, his own eyes watering. She holstered her Glock just long enough to slip Collins's arm over her shoulder while Ariel ducked under his other side. The deputy grunted, teeth clenched, but his legs twitched—enough that he could give them some help.

"Buddy," Kate told him, voice firm but warm, "I need you to take as much of your own weight as you can. Just a little. Help us get you standing. We'll do the rest."

"I'll... try," he rasped.

"Good man."

They hauled him upright—Kate under his left arm, Ariel under his right—a perfect two-person assist. Collins sagged between them, but the slight pressure of his boots on the floor made the lift doable.

His breath wheezed wetly with every step.

"Stay with us, Evan," Kate ordered, voice threaded with steel.

Smoke pushed harder into the kitchen, chasing them from behind. Ariel coughed as they staggered toward the back door.

The hallway lights flickered. A beam cracked above them. Something in the burning bedroom collapsed with a roar.

"Mom!" Ariel cried.

"I know, baby. Keep moving."

They reached the back door—and Kate's stomach dropped.

The wood frame had swollen from the heat.

The door was stuck.

"No, no, no—" Kate grabbed the knob and yanked hard. It didn't budge.

Behind them, flames snapped louder, laughing at their plight.

Kate let go of Collins for half a second—just long enough to draw her Glock—and slammed the butt of it into the doorframe, splintering soft pine. She kicked near the latch. Once. Twice.

On the third kick, the swollen seal finally cracked. She whispered quick words of thanks toward the sky above the forest.

Cold fog rushed in like mercy.

"Go!" Kate ordered.

They maneuvered Collins through the doorway, his boots dragging over the threshold. The burst of cold air hit his lungs, making him gasp, but he stayed conscious.

Outside, the world was a different kind of dark—open, fog-drenched, eerily quiet except for the low roar of the fire behind them.

Kate and Ariel half-carried, half-walked him across the damp grass, away from the smoke belching from the back windows.

"There," Kate breathed hard. Her words were punctuated by a hacking cough. "We're going to the woodpile. Just a few more steps, Deputy."

The stacked cords of oak and hickory stood shoulder-high against the shadowed north wall of the cabin, untouched by the flames. A chopping stump sat nearby, slick with dew. It blocked the line of sight to the front of the house.

Perfect cover.

They got Collins behind the woodpile and lowered him gently until his back rested against the logs. He slumped, exhausted, trembling, but alive.

Ariel crouched beside him, one hand still on his shoulder. "You okay?"

He managed a nod and attempted a smile. "Better... out here."

Kate leaned in close, cupping Ariel's cheek. "Stay right here with him. You've got the gun. Now if Logan comes near you, you shoot until he stops moving. Understand?"

Ariel nodded, tears threatening. "Mom... be careful."

"I will."

A beat.

"I promise."

Kate rose, turning toward the front yard. Smoke rose behind her in thick tendrils; the glow from Ariel's burning bedroom painted the fog in hellish orange. Ember flakes drifted past her like dying fireflies.

She could see the porch rail through the smoke.

She could feel Logan out there.

Waiting.

This was it.

Kate exhaled once—slow, steady—and moved toward the front of the house.

She had chosen her battlefield.

And she was ready.

Chapter 37

Kate rounded the corner of the cabin, boots sinking into damp earth. Smoke curled around her, warm against the cold fog, carrying the smell of burning cedar and scorched fabric — the smell of her haven and everything in it going up in flames.

Rage, cold and pure, propelled her.

The fire behind her roared higher, hungry now, crawling along the eaves. A window burst with a violent pop. Embers drifted around her like stars dying midair.

She clutched her Glock with both hands as she stepped into the front yard.

And there he was.

Logan was in the yard, limping but upright, shoulders hunched like a bull about to charge. The firelight flickered wildly, turning him into a living silhouette – broad, bleeding, feral.

His eyes locked onto hers with twisted joy.

And then he smiled.

As if this was a reunion.

As if this was a damned love story.

Kate raised the gun, sighting center mass.

"Don't take another step."

Logan tilted his head, blood running down the side of his face like war paint.

"Katie... put that thing down. You won't shoot me."

He took a step...

Then suddenly lunged.

She fired, but missed anything vital. The shot went high and caught him in the shoulder.

It cracked the fog like lightning. Logan jerked sideways with a raw howl, his shirt blooming red—but he didn't fall. It wasn't a hit with stopping power.

It was like a horror movie where the monster just keeps coming, no matter what.

He just smiled.

Twisted.

Perverse.

Something like devotion warped into a grotesque shape. The stink of fuel clung to him, burning her nose.

"You actually did it," he crowed, almost awed. "I can't believe you shot me."

He lunged again.

Kate took the next shot—too fast, too close—and her second round skimmed past him as he slammed into her with his full weight. They hit the front of the porch railing hard, the wood shuddering and cracking beneath the impact. She couldn't hold onto her gun, and it flew from her hand and clattered across the porch, vanishing into smoke and rolling embers.

"Mom!" Ariel shrieked from somewhere behind the woodpile.

She didn't have the breath to answer. The wind had been thoroughly knocked out of her. Kate thought she heard Evan say something quiet and steadying, but the world had narrowed to the man crushing the air out of her lungs.

She tried to swing.

He laughed at her feeble attempts.

She was still on her feet, pinned against the porch's remaining railing with his forearm across her chest, pressing hard enough to steal her breath. His forehead rested against hers, a grotesque parody of intimacy.

For a heartbeat, she was back in her old apartment,

face down,

helpless,

fabric pressed into her nostrils,

breath going thin —

No.

Not again.

She was not that woman anymore. She fought like a wildcat, grabbing, clawing, scratching, striking. She would *not* let him take her down to the ground . She used the railings behind her to keep herself upright.

"Katie," he hissed against her cheek, breath hot and sour, "Why do you keep fighting this?"

She snarled through clenched teeth, shoving at him. "Get the hell off me!" She went for his eyes with her thumbs, but he grabbed her hands.

He laughed— broken - breathless. "I went to prison for you, Katie. That should mean-"

Kate put a stop to his creepy declaration by driving her knee directly into his wounded thigh with every ounce of force she had.

Logan screamed, his grip faltering.

Kate twisted hard, rolling out of his hold. She scrambled backward and found herself on the front of the porch, slapped hard by smoke and heat. The air was blistering this close to the flames.

Logan staggered after her, panting, clutching his thigh, which had begun bleeding again, rage twisting his face into something barely recognizable as human.

"You wanna fight? You really think you have a chance against me?" he snarled. "Okay. Let's fight, bitch."

He advanced on her.

Slow.

Certain.

She'd finally convinced him she wanted nothing to do with him, and the result was icy, murderous rage.

Kate pawed blindly for her gun but couldn't find it through the smoke.

She was coughing...she was blinded by tears from the smoke.

She needed a weapon — anything — to even the field. Even with all her training, she knew she couldn't fight him hand-to-hand and win.

Her hand closed around something on the porch floor. A fallen two-by-four from the shattered railing—one end jagged and sharp from breaking off, the other end charred and orange from the flames licking out the windows.

She didn't think.

She didn't plan.

Kate clutched the piece of wood in both hands and jabbed at his face.

Once.

He dodged.

Twice.

She made contact, and he staggered. She got closer and swung for the fences.

The burning end connected with Logan's forearm and shoulder—a brutal, cracking thud that reverberated up her arms, numbing her hands and sending sparks scattering. She grunted from the force, but she didn't let go.

He swore.

Kept coming.

She prepared for another vicious set of jabs.

Then the flames took root – crawled up the sleeve of his jacket.

He stared down at it, bewildered—the way a child looks at a scraped knee before the pain hits.

The fire flared upward.

Logan shrieked and stumbled back, slapping uselessly at himself, spinning and choking. The accelerant he'd used to burn her cabin fed the flames in ravenous orange bursts.

He spun, flailing, choking on smoke and panic. Screaming words she couldn't understand. He hit the ground.

Kate froze.

She hadn't wanted this.

She didn't want to watch this.

"ROLL!" she screamed.

Her voice no longer sounded like her own.

"ROLL ON THE GROUND!"

He didn't.

Whether he couldn't hear her or simply refused to listen, she didn't know.

He crawled toward her, reaching for her even as flames climbed his shoulder and neck.

"Katie—"

His voice broke into a tortured gurgle that ended in a scream. She would never forget how horrible it sounded as long as she lived.

Kate moved without thinking. She ripped the porch curtain down from the side that was not yet engulfed in flames and ran at him.

Her instincts were screaming at her to save even him, because she was human and he was burning alive.

It wasn't supposed to end like this.

It wasn't supposed to be another horrifying moment that was with her forever.

She pressed the curtain to his shoulder, shoving down hard, trying to wrap it around him. The flames only flared hotter, racing along the fabric.

"Kate—Katie—PLEASE—"

His voice was barely human now. Deep. Animalistic. Soon, the sounds that emerged had no meaning.

Somehow, he still grabbed for her and caught her wrist in an iron grip—wild, blind—and the fire jumped.

She stumbled back. She tore free, chest heaving, eyes burning from smoke and horror, ripping her jacket off before it fully ignited, barely feeling her own skin burn.

She watched in dismay as he staggered farther away, half running, half collapsing, until he crashed into burning debris spilling from the window.

Logan fell to his knees.

Screamed once.

Twice.

Fire met fire and swallowed him whole.

Then...nothing.

Kate stood trembling in her front yard, one hand pressed to her mouth, tears carving hot tracks down her soot-streaked cheeks.

It was over.

Finally over.

Footsteps crunched across the grass behind her.

"Mom?"

Ariel.

Kate turned, and Ariel ran straight into her arms, sobbing.

Kate held her tight, burying her face in her daughter's hair. "I'm here," she whispered. "It's okay. You're safe. You're safe. It's over."

From behind the woodpile, Collins rasped hoarsely, "He down?"

Kate nodded, still holding Ariel. "He's gone."

Together, they moved back toward the injured deputy.

Far through the smoke and fog, sirens wailed—faint but growing.

Kate collapsed to her knees with Ariel, overwhelmed and shaking, the fire at their backs lighting the night like the end of the world.

Haven Hill was burning.

Logan was dead.

And in the ashes, Kate finally felt the first fragile flicker of safety she'd known in years.

Chapter 38

Kate stayed kneeling in the grass with Ariel curled against her chest, both of them shaking, both of them watching the inferno that had once been Haven Hill. They were still too close to the house, but they didn't want to leave Deputy Collins, nor did they want to make him get up again when help was so near.

The sirens grew louder—rising and falling through the fog, the sort of sound that once would have filled her with relief. Now it only made her feel hollow. Untethered. Those sounds had no business out in the forest.

Blue and red lights finally strobed through the tree-line. Two patrol cars. A fire engine. Then another. An ambulance was behind them. Tires skidded on wet gravel as they pulled into the clearing.

The whole county was coming.

Shadows spilled out—uniforms, helmets, reflective tape catching firelight.

"Sheriff's department!" a voice ordered. "Call out! Hands where we can see them!"

Kate emerged from behind the woodpile, lifting one trembling arm, the other still wrapped around Ariel.

"Over here!" she called, voice rough with smoke. "Officer down! Officer down!"

Flashlights speared through the fog. Two deputies sprinted toward her, weapons drawn until they saw Ariel clinging to her, soot-streaked and sobbing. One of them knelt in front of Kate, eyes going wide at the sight of the blood that soaked her shirt all the way through to her skin.

"Holy- ...uh, ma'am, are you hurt?"

Kate shook her head. "Not me. It's not my blood. Deputy Collins—behind the woodpile—he needs help now. Chest wound, abdominal wound, shock."

"Go!" the deputy barked to his partner.

More figures approached – EMTs pulling gear bags, rolling gurneys, firefighters rushing hoses toward the burning cabin. So many noises that didn't belong in the forest.

Ariel finally peeled away from Kate long enough to cling to one of her arms. "Is it really over?" she whispered.

Kate stroked her daughter's hair, shaking but steady. "Yeah, baby. It's over. He's gone."

A paramedic—mid-fifties, silver beard, kind eyes—stooped beside them. "Ma'am, can you stand?"

"Of course I can stand. I'm fine," Kate insisted.

The paramedic took one look at her dilated pupils, the soot smeared across her face, the trembling in her hands. "No, ma'am, you're not."

But Kate brushed him off.

Collins.

She needed to know.

She limped toward the woodpile, careful not to get in the EMTs' way.

Two EMTs were already working on him behind the woodpile, calling vitals, applying oxygen, checking the chest seal she'd placed. One of them sounded startled.

"This was done right," he said.

"Better than right," the other agreed. "She bought EMS time, or what?"

"He has a wife," Kate told them hoarsely. "And a daughter."

Both EMTs looked up at her with something like respect.

"Then let's get him back to them," one said, and they lifted Collins onto a stretcher.

"Collins? Evan?" she leaned over him.

He opened his eyes, met hers, and nodded slightly.

"Thank you for keeping my Ariel safe. I can never repay you."

Collins pulled the oxygen mask down. "Thank you," he rasped, "for getting me back to my girls."

Their hands clasped for a moment, bonded by the trauma and fear they had endured together. Kate let go of his hand, and the paramedics hurried him toward the first ambulance that had arrived.

A firefighter jogged over. "Ma'am? We're trying to get a handle on the fire, but I need to know—is anyone still inside?"

"No," Kate said quietly. "Just... things." She stopped. Her throat tightened, and tears slipped down her soot-covered cheeks.

Just the memories.

Just the haven she'd built.

The firefighter nodded grimly and rushed away.

A tall, imposing man in a crisp deputy's uniform approached her, stepping carefully, respectful of the scene.

"Ma'am? I'm Sergeant Dempsey. We have units en route to secure the perimeter. The man responsible—is he...?"

Wordlessly, Kate pointed toward the wreckage of the porch. Logan had been reduced to a hunk of smoldering debris beside the cabin.

Dempsey followed her gaze.

The expression on his face shifted, darkened. "Understood."

"Sergeant?" Kate called as he turned away. "There's another victim. Mr. Lavern Slocum—our next-door neighbor. I can get you into his house."

Another deputy approached, lowering his voice. "We'll need statements once EMS clears you."

Kate nodded numbly.

Paramedics loaded Collins into the ambulance with practiced urgency. The doors slammed, and the vehicle began easing around the cluster of emergency responders.

Ariel let out a shaky breath. "Mom... can we follow them to make sure Deputy Collins is okay?"

Kate kissed her temple. "We're going, too."

The paramedic from earlier gestured. "Ma'am, we'll take you both in the second ambulance. Evaluation only. No argument."

Kate opened her mouth to argue, then closed it. She was swaying. Her body had started to shut down the moment the danger passed, adrenaline draining out of her like blood from a cut artery.

"Okay," she whispered as her knees folded. Sergeant Dempsey caught her before she hit the ground, and Ariel stood in staunch support.

Firefighters shouted behind her as another section of the roof collapsed in a burst of sparks.

Despite her wobbly legs, Kate refused to get on a stretcher. She would get out of here under her own steam. Ariel clung to her waist as they stepped toward the ambulance. Deputies guided them over the uneven ground, gentle hands under each elbow.

At the open back doors, she turned for one final look.

Haven Hill was collapsing inward, flames licking at what remained of the rafters. The wind carried burning pine needles like fireflies scattering into the fog.

She waited for grief to hit her—the sharp, crushing kind.

But what she felt instead was something quieter.

A strange lightness in her chest.

A beginning.

She climbed into the ambulance with Ariel as the doors swung shut behind them, blocking the view of the inferno that had once been her haven.

It had been a haven, she thought. The place had sheltered them and kept them safe through the most horrifying of circumstances.

Maybe that had been its purpose all along.

The ambulance jolted forward, sirens drowning out any possibility of conversation. Kate tightened her arm around Ariel. Haven Hill burned behind them, shrinking into fog. Ahead lay lights, questions, answers — the aftermath. The part no one ever prepares for.

Chapter 39

The ambulance smelled of plastic and old coffee and antiseptic.

Kate sat on the bench seat, Ariel glued to her side. She didn't need to lie down. She was fine.

A paramedic clipped something to Kate's finger; it pinched slightly. A strap went around her arm. Cuff inflating, tightening on bruises she didn't even know she had. She winced, and the paramedic loosened the cuff a little. The sound of the Velcro was startling.

"Blood pressure's elevated," someone said.

"No kidding," Kate rasped.

Ariel's hand was small and hot in hers. Too tight. Clinging.

"Sweetheart," the paramedic said gently to Ariel, "I'm just going to listen to your chest, okay? Nice big breaths for me."

Ariel nodded and obeyed, eyes never leaving Kate's face.

Kate watched the lightbar strobe past the back windows, red-blue-red-blue, and even though the vehicle she was in wasn't moving, she felt carsick. Why did she feel carsick when she was sitting still?

She began to heave into a bag the paramedic held under her face until her stomach was empty. Then she began to shake. She shook so hard her teeth were rattling against themselves uncontrollably.

"Ma'am, you need to lie down for the ride."

"No, I'm fine," she argued weakly, wiping her mouth on her sleeve.

Then hands were on her shoulders, the world tipped backward, and she was suddenly lying down whether she wanted to be or not.

Then they were lifting her gurney out of the ambulance, and Ariel wasn't holding her hand anymore.

She reached out for her, but the people wheeling her in kept tucking her arm back onto the gurney.

...

The lights were fluorescent and loud.

Voices overlapped like a flurry of birds—nurses, EMTs, disembodied overhead pages. Someone cut Kate's sleeve up the seam. Someone else pressed something cool to her face.

"Any chest pain? Shortness of breath? Lightheaded? Where do you hurt?"

"Just... everywhere," Kate said.

Ariel sat on the gurney beside hers, blanket around her shoulders, looking very small and very old at the same time.

A nurse shone a penlight into Ariel's eyes. "You hit your head at all, sweetie? Any dizziness? Nausea?"

Ariel swallowed. "No. I'm okay. It's my mom you should be worried about."

Kate tried to snort, but it came out as a cough.

"Vitals are actually decent," another nurse muttered, glancing at Kate's monitor. "She's just fried."

"She nearly had a house burn down around her," the first nurse said. "Fried is appropriate."

They hooked Kate to a portable monitor anyway. Checked her ribs. Pain so sharp she cried out. It hadn't hurt there until they touched it. They palpated her bruised shoulder and wanted X-rays. She refused until they said Ariel could go with her.

Ariel sat up straight in a wheelchair, leading the procession to the X-ray department. Kate could look up and see she was still there.

"You two a package deal?" the tech asked lightly as he swapped the plates.

"Pretty much," Kate said.

...

They peeled Kate out of her soot-streaked clothes and into a thin hospital gown. Someone put her boots in a biohazard bag; someone else tagged Ariel's hoodie as "evidence."

Gloves snapped. Questions came in bursts.

"Any allergies?"

"Any medications?"

"Last tetanus shot?"

Kate looked at them blankly. She was thinking of the answers but couldn't quite make them come out of her mouth. What was wrong with her mouth?

A young doctor with tired eyes listened to her lungs and looked at her X-rays, raising them up to the light-box. "A little smoke irritation," he said. "We'll give you a breathing treatment and some fluids, keep an eye on you."

"I'm fine," Kate insisted. "My daughter—"

"Her stats are beautiful," the doctor said, glancing at the monitor above Ariel's bed. "She's a healthy kid in a bad situation. You're both safe here."

Safe.

The word landed and slid off, not quite sticking.

...

Somebody must have called psych or social work, because a woman in soft clothes and flat shoes appeared, clipboard tucked against her chest like a shield.

"I'm Dana," she said. Her voice was pitched high, but it wasn't shrill. It was pleasing, almost childlike. "I'm here to make sure you two have what you need that's not medical. Clothes. Phone calls. That sort of thing."

Kate looked at her blankly.

What she needed was her cabin back. Her pantry. Her porch. Her quiet.

What she needed was for Logan to never have existed in their lives.

"We're fine," Kate repeated.

Dana glanced at the band on Kate's wrist, the dried blood still ghosting her hairline, the tremor she was trying to hide.

"Of course," Dana said gently. "I'll just sit for a bit, then."

She pulled up a chair and didn't ask any questions. She just... existed in the corner, calm and unthreatening, while a respiratory therapist fitted Kate with a mask and started a nebulizer that tasted like chemical mint and plastic.

Ariel wrinkled her nose. "You sound like Darth Vader."

Kate puffed the medicated mist and managed a weak smile around the mask. "Luke, I am your father," she rasped.

Ariel snorted, a tiny, broken sound that was still a laugh.

Dana watched the exchange and scribbled something on her clipboard.

...

Time got weird.

There were IV bags. Plastic cups of water. A tray with crackers Ariel didn't touch. A tiny carton of apple juice, she did.

A nurse came in with a syringe.

"What's that?" Kate asked, instantly alert.

"Just something to help her nervous system dial down," the nurse said. "A low-dose sedative. She's shaking nonstop. It's not meant to knock her out, just to... let her rest."

Kate looked at Ariel.

Ariel's eyes were big, pupils still blown. "Will it make me dumb?" she whispered.

"No," Kate said. "Just sleepy. Like when you used to take Benadryl for allergies."

"Will you be here when I wake up?" Ariel asked.

Kate's throat closed. She swallowed hard. "I'm not going anywhere. Come on up with me."

Ariel nodded, small and brave. "Okay, then."

She crawled up onto Kate's bed, and the nurse pushed the medication into the IV port. Within minutes, Ariel's shoulders loosened. Her jaw unclenched.

Her hand stayed in Kate's, even as her eyelids grew heavy.

"You did so good," Kate whispered, brushing hair off her forehead. "So brave. So smart."

Ariel mumbled something that sounded like, "You too, Mom," and drifted under.

...

The machines beeped for a while. Kate breathed medicated air.

Ariel slept, stirring slightly at the distant wail of somebody else's pain somewhere down the hall.

Then a man in plain clothes stepped quietly into the curtained-off area, hat in his hands.

Not Dempsey. Another one. Older. Lines around his eyes.

"Hello, ma'am? May I come in for a minute?" he asked.

"Yeah, if you call me Kate."

"Kate, then. I'm Detective Rios. I know you've been through hell today. I'm not here to take a full statement right now. I just need to clarify a couple of details while they're fresh. The rest can wait until tomorrow or the next day." Rios sounded like he came from the hills, the soft twang that blended his words together in a calming melange.

"Tomorrow," Kate repeated, as if the concept was exotic.

He nodded. "Whenever you're ready. We can even come to you."

He asked about weapons. About how many shots she fired. About whether Logan said anything before the fire. Kate answered as best she could, piecing the night together in clipped phrases.

"He set Ariel's room on fire," she said, voice flat.

Rios's jaw tightened. "Intentionally?"

"As intentionally as you strike a match," Kate said. "He wanted us either smoked out or roasted."

Rios wrote that down. His pen moved more slowly on that line.

"And he died in the fire?" he asked finally.

Kate saw the flames licking up Logan's jacket, the way he'd reached for her even while he burned. The sound he'd made when he fell.

"He died from the fire," Kate corrected.

"What do you mean?"

"I didn't mean to light him—he pushed me—I swung a piece of the railing, it was burning—and then he was burning... I just wanted... to stop him... to make him stop coming... but he was on fire. I tried to smother the flames, but I couldn't."

She gasped, feeling sick as she remembered his screams. She looked around the room frantically for a moment. Ariel was still there, sleeping.

Rios waited patiently while she collected herself. Didn't rush her.

Then he met her eyes and didn't look away. "I want you to hear this as clear as I can say it, Kate: You did what you had to do to protect yourself and your daughter. From everything I can see, this was self-defense. We're not looking at you as a suspect. We're looking at you as a survivor."

Survivor.

She wasn't sure she liked that word either.

Still, she nodded. "Okay."

He left a card on the rolling table beside her water cup. "If you remember anything else, call me. Any time."

She slid the card under the edge of her phone. Evidence that the world outside the forest existed.

...

Later—minutes, hours, she wasn't sure—a nurse came to unhook Kate from the monitors.

"Your lungs sound better," the nurse said. "IV fluids are in. I thought you might want to try walking a bit."

"Okay," Kate agreed.

The nurse hesitated. "They just brought Deputy Collins out of surgery. He's still critical, but the surgeon said the family can sit in the waiting area. His wife is out there now. I thought you might want to know."

Kate's heart did a strange, painful lurch.

"Is he..." She couldn't make herself say "okay" again. That word had failed her too often.

"He's still here," the nurse said simply. "That's more than he would've been if you hadn't done what you did."

Dana, the social worker, reappeared with two sets of soft scrubs and a pair of socks for each of them. "So you don't have to keep living in paper gowns," she said.

"Thank you," Kate said gratefully.

Kate changed in the tiny bathroom. She was shocked when she saw her face in the mirror above the sink.

Soot was streaked around her face where it had been wiped but not yet thoroughly washed. Blood was dried in her hair on one side, and a nasty gash drew an abrupt line across her forehead. Her eyes were bloodshot, and the socket around the right one was swollen and purple. Her lips were dry and split. She barely recognized herself.

She scrubbed blood and soot from her face with a damp washcloth until the water in the basin swirled gray and pink. She pulled on the scrubs. They were a size too big and pale blue, and they felt like someone else's life.

Ariel stirred when Kate came back.

"Hey," Kate whispered. "How are you doing?"

"Floaty," Ariel murmured. "Like... pool noodle floaty."

"Good," Kate said. "You earned floaty."

"I dreamed the cabin wasn't real," Ariel added. "But you were."

Kate's chest hurt in a completely different way. "I like that dream."

A nurse offered a wheelchair; Kate refused.

"If I can stand, I can walk," she said.

She helped Ariel into the other set of scrubs, knotted the drawstring of her pants, pulled socks over her feet. Together, they shuffled out into the hallway, IV pole clattering alongside Ariel like a clumsy metal companion.

...

The surgical waiting room was too bright, too clean. A muted TV played a cooking show nobody was watching. A Keurig burbled in the corner. Someone's half-finished cup of coffee sat cooling on a side table.

A woman sat in one of the vinyl chairs, hands white-knuckled around a tissue. Early thirties, maybe. Dark hair pulled back in a messy bun. Tear tracks shiny on her cheeks. She was alone.

Ariel's fingers tightened around Kate's.

"That's Evan's wife, isn't it?" Ariel whispered.

Kate swallowed. Her throat was suddenly dry.

"We don't have to—" she began.

"Yes, we do," Ariel said quietly.

They approached slowly, not wanting to startle her.

"Mrs. Collins?" Kate queried softly.

The woman stood so quickly that the tissue fluttered to the floor. "Yes. Are you—did you—"

"I'm Kate, and this is my daughter Ariel. Your husband... Evan... he came to help us." Her voice wobbled, but she pushed through. "If he hadn't... I don't think we'd be standing here."

For a moment, Mrs. Collins just stared at her, as if that sentence had too many pieces to process.

Then her face crumpled.

"You're the ones from the cabin," she whispered.

Kate nodded, suddenly riddled with guilt.

Ariel said, "He was really brave."

Mrs. Collins put her hand to her chest for a moment, then looked at Kate. "They said some... woman at the scene put something on his chest and stopped the bleeding in his belly and..." Her voice trembled. "Was that you?"

Kate wanted to say it wasn't enough. That it might still not be enough. Instead, she nodded once. "I did what I could with what I had."

Mrs. Collins's eyes filled. She reached out, hesitated, then took Kate's hand in both of hers.

"Thank you," she whispered. "Whatever happens... thank you for giving him a chance."

Kate's vision blurred. "He saved us first."

Ariel slipped around Kate and hugged the deputy's wife.

They sat together after that.

Not talking much.

Just breathing the same recycled air, listening for footsteps in the hall, watching for a surgeon's silhouette in the doorway.

Kate leaned back in the chair, Ariel's head on her shoulder, and stared at the floor tiles until they blurred into abstract shapes. Her body ached. Her eyes burned.

But nobody was pounding on her door.

Nobody was in the woods.

No one was watching her cabin.

There was no cabin.

Just this bright, too-cold room and the person she loved more than anyone in the world sitting within arm's reach.

Kate exhaled, slow and shaky.

For the first time in years, when she scanned for danger... her mind didn't automatically fill in Logan's shadow.

It felt wrong.

It felt empty.

It felt... possible.

She reached over and took Ariel's hand in one of hers and, without fully realizing she was doing it, reached for Mrs. Collins's hand with the other.

They sat like that in a quiet little chain,

three women —

one of them just barely reaching that title —

breathing in and out –

waiting to see what the world would look like on the other side of the longest night of their lives.

Epilogue

They came back to the site of the cabin a month later.

That felt soon to anyone who hadn't lived through it, but Kate knew waiting longer would only make it harder. Ash settles. Weather moves things. Animals scatter what's useful. If there was anything worth saving, now was the time.

The road up Haven Hill was still passable, though the county had blocked off the final stretch beyond the clearing. Kate parked where the temporary barrier stood and shut off the engine.

Neither of them spoke at first.

The cabin was gone.

Not "burned," not "ruined" — gone. Reduced to a low scatter of ash, warped metal, and foundation stones that marked where walls had once stood. The air no longer smelled like smoke. That was almost worse. It smelled like wet soil and winter, like the mountain had already moved on.

Ariel got out of the truck and stood still, hands shoved into her jacket pockets.

"It looks smaller," she said.

Kate nodded. "It always does afterward."

They walked the perimeter first. Kate's habit. Boundaries before details. The fire had stayed mostly contained to the structure, scorching the surrounding ground but sparing the trees. The forest had taken the hit and kept standing.

Good mountain, she thought.

"Be careful around the basement – it's just a big hole with no stairs now," cautioned Kate.

She knelt near what had once been the kitchen and brushed ash aside with a gloved hand.

Metal clinked softly.

The cast-iron skillet emerged blackened but intact, handle scorched, weight unchanged. Kate tested it, then set it carefully aside.

"Still good," she said.

Ariel nodded, unsurprised. "Of course it is. This is why preppers love cast iron."

They worked methodically after that.

The fireproof document box was half-buried but sealed. The latch resisted, then popped open. Everything inside was untouched.

Ariel exhaled slowly.

"That would've been bad," she said.

"Yes," Kate agreed. "It would've."

They found smaller things, too.

A compass, clouded but working.

One of Kate's knives, heat-discolored but straight.

The Glock was gone. Melted, probably. Kate didn't look long for it.

The parts of a metal windchime remained, though all the strings that had held it together burned.

She stood and surveyed the clearing again, committing it to memory in a different way now. Not as a place to sleep. Not as shelter.

Just as ground.

"We'll take what matters," she said. "The rest stays."

Ariel picked up a warped metal frog magnet — it had been on the refrigerator — and turned it over in her hand.

"This?" she asked.

Kate laughed. "Obviously."

They loaded what they could into the truck. Not much, but enough. When they were done, Kate walked the foundation one last time, slow and deliberate, the way you close a door even when there's no house left to lock.

"Okay," she said finally.

Ariel climbed into the passenger seat.

As they drove away, the clearing disappeared behind the trees, quiet and unremarkable again.

Haven Hill wasn't just a cabin. It was the mountain. The land, the forests, the creek had sheltered them when it mattered most.

Haven Hill had done its job and earned its name.

....

Six months later, things at Haven Hill had changed again.

Kate had been stunned to receive a large envelope from a lawyer's office informing her that their dear Mr. Slocum had left his property to her. It made her cry all over again for their beloved neighbor.

She was still talking to a therapist about that terrifying weekend when she and Ariel had both nearly died. She felt guilty about gaining property when it seemed as though Mr. Slocum's death had been her fault. She'd finally begun to accept it as a beautiful gift and was using her insurance money from the old cabin to renovate the Slocum place.

In late May, the mountain was green again in that deep, settled way that meant winter was truly gone. The gravel drive had been graded. The porch was rebuilt stronger than before. The house itself was a delightful combination of Slocum — plain, sturdy, unpretentious — and theirs now: a splash of color here, a goofy frog magnet there.

They went up on Memorial Day weekend – Ariel had a long weekend off from school. On Sunday, they planned to entertain before heading back to the city.

Kate had gone to get more ice. She returned, parking her old yellow Jeep beneath the big oak that shaded the west side of the house. She shut off the engine and sat for a moment, listening.

Laughter. The clink of metal. A radio was playing low somewhere near the fire pit.

Life, continuing.

Their guests had arrived while she was out, and Ariel had made them feel welcome.

The firepit had been cleared and reset, stones stacked carefully, ash raked neat. A rustic wooden table stood nearby, laden with coolers and foil-covered trays. There was potato salad and far too many hot dogs for the number of tummies they were meant to feed.

Deputy Collins sat in a camp chair near the fire. He moved more slowly now, and he was careful when he stood, but for the most part, he had healed from his encounter at Kate's former cabin.

When he spotted her, he smiled.

"Hey," he said. "You've got ice!"

Kate nodded. "What would a barbecue be without cold drinks?"

He stood with effort, not rushing it, and extended a hand. They shook. Solid. Brief.

"You look good," he said.

"You look... upright," Kate replied, laughing.

He huffed a laugh. "High praise."

His wife came over then, carrying paper plates, her expression softer than it had been when Kate had seen her in the hospital waiting room. Less brittle. No longer terrified. She gave Kate a bright smile, then directed her attention toward Ariel and the Collins's daughter, Olivia.

"Hey, young ladies, out of the Rice Krispie treats!" she pretended to scold the girls. "Dessert means you guys eat real food before dessert."

"Yes, ma'am," Ariel said solemnly, already edging toward the trees and motioning Olivia to follow. They had a wide age gap – Ariel was 15 now, and Olivia was only 9, but the forest had a way of bringing people together.

Kate watched her go — not with fear, exactly, but with awareness. The kind that doesn't fade. She didn't resent it anymore.

After they ate, someone suggested heading down to the creek.

It wasn't a long drive. Just a rough spur road and a short walk through trees. The creek cut through the lower part of the adjoining land where the old cabin once stood, cold and clear, fed by snowmelt and spring rain.

The kids went first, splashing carefully, laughing when the water shocked their ankles. Shoes stayed on. Boundaries were set and respected without challenge.

Kate stood back with Evan and his wife, watching.

"She's doing good," Evan said quietly.

Kate nodded. "She is."

"So are you," he added.

Kate didn't answer right away. She looked up the slope, toward where the old cabin clearing lay hidden by distance and trees. She didn't feel the pull to go there anymore. That surprised her, but she accepted it.

"Haven Hill didn't end," she said finally. "It just... changed shape."

Collins followed her gaze. "Seems like it does that."

They stood in companionable silence for a while, listening to the creek and the kids and the mountain being exactly what it had always been.

Later, when they drove back up to Slocum's house, the sun was beginning to dip, the light warm and slanted. Someone lit the fire again. Another person passed around marshmallows.

Kate sat on the porch steps, Ariel beside her, shoulders touching.

"This is still Haven Hill," Ariel said, as if reading her thoughts.

Kate smiled, small but real. "Yeah. It is."

The mountain didn't care about structures.

It never had.

And as the evening settled in around them — smoke rising, voices low, the creek whispering below — Kate understood something clearly, finally:

They hadn't lost their refuge.

They had learned how to carry it with them.

About the Author

Daisy Luther is a well-traveled, coffee-swigging blogger and author who lives in urban North Carolina. She is the founder and publisher of TheOrganicPrepper.com, a popular blog. Daisy is the best-selling author of 17 non-fiction books. Haven Hill is her second work of fiction.